Sunshine and Second Chances

Kim Nash

Prologue

Olivia

'SUPER, THANKS SO much. Can't wait!'

Olivia ended the call, threw down the phone on the sofa behind her and took a deep breath. There was no turning back now.

She'd been dreaming about this moment for so long; never sure if it would happen. But now it really was. It wouldn't be long before they were all back together.

Apprehensive, but excited, she knew she'd have some time to herself and some space to work out what the future held for her. Only four weeks to wait till the big day.

Chapter One

'WILL YOU GET a bloody move on. For God's sake!'

'Coming, Mum!' Seb ambled down the stairs, not a rush in him.

'Sebastian! *Hurry up!* It's *your* football training that we're going to, not mine. Do you think for once in your life, you can get ready without all this last-minute dashing around? Have you got your water bottle?' She knew he hadn't because she'd seen it on his bedside table when she went in to wake him up and he didn't have it in his hand.

'Where are my football boots, Mum?' He scratched his head and frowned.

'I don't know, Seb, they're *your* boots not mine.'

Spectacularly rolling his eyes, Sebastian huffed as he turned back towards his room at a snail's pace. Olivia was getting more stressed by the minute. Once again they were going to be late through no fault of her own. Everything seemed such a rush these days, and she wanted some calm in her life. Surely that wasn't too much to ask for.

She'd spent the last fifteen minutes, on and off, yelling up the stairs to her younger son, telling him he had to get his kit on, which she'd already laid out on his bed to make life easier for him. He kept saying he was, but then when she went to give him a final call and tell him they were going to be late – she had to go up because he wasn't answering her – he was still sitting in his pants playing on his Xbox because he was 'just finishing his game'. She loved him with all her heart, but he was so infuriating at times.

Talking of infuriating, while she was waiting downstairs, her elder son, James, wandered in from the kitchen, his dressing gown half on and half off, still half asleep, eating a piece of toast and dropping crumbs all over the hall floor. Olivia sighed. Why couldn't he just get a plate? These boys would be the death of her, they really would.

She closed her eyes and counted to three and smiled. 'We'll be back after football, so we'll only be gone a few hours, darling.'

'Take a chill pill, Mum. I'll be fine. I'm fourteen, I'm practically an adult.'

Only when it suits you, Olivia thought to herself. Most of the time he acted very much like a child still.

'Wait for me, darling!' came a yell from the kitchen, followed by her husband, George, clattering into the hall dragging his golf clubs behind him. 'You can drop me off at the club on the way. Then I can have a few beers with the boys when I've finished, and I'll call you when I'm ready to be picked up.'

No *would you mind?* No *please*. It was just expected of her. Plus diverting to the golf club was going to make them even later.

'Oh and by the way, the dog has done a really runny poo on the kitchen floor. Not sure what you've been feeding him. That'll need clearing up, darling.'

Olivia could have cried. Another job that had been left to her. If she stopped to do it now there would be no point going out because they'd miss the game, so right now she needed to get them out of the house. She'd have to clear up the mess when she got back. She slammed the front door behind her and stomped the fifteen or so paces to the car – as much as a gravel drive allowed you to stomp when you were wearing heels.

The engine of the week-old Jaguar four-wheel drive roared into life and she revved it a few times, trying to attract the attention of the various members of her family. But much to her annoyance, and after yet another couple of minutes, Seb sauntered out in his socks with his football boots in his hands. As he jumped in the back of the car she turned around to make sure he was belted in. His beautiful blue eyes and angelic ten-year-old face smiled at her, a smile that lit up his face, and the corners of her lips twitched.

George then ambled out, the phone to his ear, barking instructions to who she presumed was his secretary, Cynthia. Poor woman, she had Olivia's every sympathy having to pander to George's whims every day. That was why Olivia bought her a relaxing spa day for her Christmas present every year. No one deserved it more. George threw her new Mulberry handbag, which had been sitting on the passenger seat, onto the floor and she used her counting-to-three tactic for the umpteenth time that morning, before she put the car into gear and drove out through the remote-control gates towards the main road.

She glanced back in the wing mirrors, at their gorgeous barn conversion, and thought that she should probably be more grateful, and feel lucky for what she had. But she had never felt more exhausted and worn down in her life.

Once she'd dropped George at the golf club and Seb at football training, while she knew she should probably be dashing round Waitrose with a shopping trolley, she instead went to the nearest coffee shop and sank into a big squishy armchair with a huge caramel latte and a lemon muffin and gave a sigh of relief. She couldn't wait for the break in Portugal with the girls. She loved her family dearly, but they were so demanding and needy, and she really was reaching the end of her tether.

Motherhood was the best job in the world at times, giving the most amazing rewards, and the love she felt for her family was sometimes overwhelming. But oh boy, did it drive her bonkers too. For once in their lives they were going to have to man up and cope without her.

Chapter Two

SAMANTHA WAS DOING her best to keep busy since he'd gone, but she was struggling with it all, to be honest. She'd never felt as alone as she did right now. There was a void that she didn't think she'd ever be able to fill. She knew it was still early days and that she had a huge adjustment to make in her life, and that she'd get through it, but it was definitely going to take some getting used to.

It was the quietness she couldn't bear. Their house used to be full of life, with a steady flow of friends coming and going, and she was always busy keeping them supplied with food and drink. It was a total contrast to the complete silence of now and that made her feel so sad. And so lonesome. Minutes seemed like hours and there were times when she could go for days without seeing anyone. Over the years, her friends had dwindled away, she'd never really needed anyone else apart from her small but perfectly formed family, who she loved and wanted to spend her time making happy.

But now everything had changed. She had a huge gaping hole in her heart and she had no idea how to fill it.

She flicked on the iron in the spare room. She had to do something to keep herself busy before she drove herself insane, so she decided she may as well iron the few clothes that were sitting in the laundry basket. Coming across a top of Peter's, she pulled it close to her nose, inhaling his scent, which was still evident even though the shirt had been washed. Opening the door of his bedroom, the smell of teenage boy hit her, a mix of musky deodorant, food and stinky old trainers, and she flung open the window. It didn't matter how long he'd been gone, it still smelt the same. How did boys manage to do that? While she wanted to freshen up the room, she never wanted to forget that smell. Her darling boy.

She popped the T-shirt in the top drawer of the tallboy in the corner and, as she turned, caught sight of herself in the full-length mirror. Lank-looking hair with roots that desperately needed some attention, tied back in a bobble, a face free of make-up – because what was the point if she never saw anyone? – and a tatty old T-shirt and leggings. Her shoulders slumped. She looked and felt grey and miserable. She had never felt more down in the mouth.

She knew that she had needed a kick up the backside to kick-start her life for a long while, and even though some of her was dreading it, perhaps a holiday in the sun, with the love of her friends and some laughter therapy, was just what she needed. A bit of a tan on her body, some warmth on her skin, and she might be able to recharge her very depleted batteries. Perhaps then she'd feel a little more like the Samantha of the past. That Samantha had been full of fun and ambition and hope for the future, before the devastating events of her life had worn her down. Perhaps it was time that the Samantha of old made a reappearance.

Remembering that she'd put some holiday clothes away a couple of years ago, she opened the loft hatch on the landing and pulled down the ladder. She tentatively climbed up – it was the first time she'd ever done it without someone holding the bottom – and feeling both brave and vulnerable, she felt around for the light switch to the right of the hatch. Ah, there it was. Treading carefully on the joists, she spied the purple flowery case she was looking for hidden behind a chest. She opened it up and smiled when she saw clothes she'd not seen in years, each item holding different memories. Some really needed to go to the charity shop, but there were others that would be perfect for a few days away in the sun.

Thinking about the holiday made her feel anxious. It had been years since she'd seen the girls properly. They'd kept in touch for a long while, seen each other a few times, but had drifted off as their lives took different directions and they'd moved to various parts of the country. While they didn't live a million miles from each other, they were far enough away that a real effort had to be made to meet up. It wasn't like they could nip out for a coffee every now and again, as they might have done had they have lived closer.

Trust Olivia to remember that stupid bloody pact they'd made on that holiday when they were celebrating their twenty-first birthday year: that they would get together when they had all either hit, or were about to hit, the big FIVE ZERO!

How the hell had she become fifty? Life had flown by and it was weird being this age because you were kind of over halfway through your life. What a depressing thought. Especially now that she was entirely on her own. Just lately, she'd been feeling like her life was over already. This was not the way her younger self would have imagined her being at this age.

Her phone pinged and her heart leapt as she checked her messages, but it was only the local butcher letting her know what offers were on that week. Her heart sank deeper than before. It had been an hour since she'd sent the text but there had been no response. This wasn't unusual but it was annoying. It was Saturday so he should be around. She'd managed to get herself worked up into a real state before she sent the text, trying to be chatty and casual, not too needy, but she did need answers to settle her mind. She'd read and rewritten it three times before she was happy with what she'd sent, but still nothing had come back. It would probably be hours before there was a response. Even days. That had happened before too.

She really needed to get a life and stop dwelling on things and vowed to make the most of the week in Portugal. This holiday could be a huge turning point in her life, but only if she let it be.

Chapter Three

WELL, WHEN THERE are two egg custards in the pack, and you live alone, surely they expect you to eat them both, thought Debs to herself as she crammed the last bit of the second one in her mouth.

Feeling way too full, and undoing the button on her jeans, she wished now that she'd put on her joggers. Who even invented joggers, anyway? Ironically, those who jogged didn't bloody need elasticated-waisted trousers.

She felt so guilty for what she'd done, and what she seemed to be doing a lot lately, but it was almost as if food had become an obsession with her. She knew that she was overweight, and really wanted to do something about it, yet didn't seem able, even though her doctor had warned her that she was in a health danger zone. It was almost as if because she was bigger now than she'd ever been and because she believed she'd never be able to put it right, she just ate what she wanted and thought, what the hell to the consequences. Sometimes, even when she felt so full after she'd eaten something, determined not to leave a morsel, it was almost as if she was testing her body to see just how far she could go before something drastic happened.

She'd felt so bad about herself since Dave left. He'd said that she'd let herself go and had put on a ton of weight, and wasn't the same woman that he had married fifteen years ago. In fairness, he hadn't been bald with a cauliflower ear, smelly feet and a beer belly when she'd met him, so it wasn't only she who was guilty of changing. But one evening he'd sat her down and told her that he didn't love her any more, and that he had been spending time with someone else and fallen in love. Debs' jaw had dropped to the floor when he'd revealed that it was Penny from three doors down. The fact that he now lived there had devastated her. She'd known Penny since she'd moved into their close a couple of years earlier and had always thought she was really nice. They'd even been in each other's houses for coffee during that time. She'd thought they were friends. Some friend she turned out to be.

Debs was really hit hard when she'd bumped into them last week in Tesco. It was typical that her trolley was full of cakes, bread and chocolate, and theirs was full of salad, fruit and vegetables. Dave just looked in her trolley and tutted at her, and Penny – who the girls on a Skype call one night had nicknamed Perfect Fucking Penny or PFP for short – smiled sweetly and swung her perfect blonde-highlighted ponytail in the opposite direction and sashayed off down the aisle.

Debs had stared at her peachy, tiny backside in tight multi-coloured leggings and couldn't help but admire her flat stomach and six pack which were clearly visible in the vest top she was wearing as she reached on tiptoe to grab something from the top shelf. Debs realised that her own figure hadn't looked like that since she'd been about twelve. She'd wrapped her baggy grey cardigan further around her body and her cheeks had burned, and she'd wished she'd made more of an effort that morning instead of grabbing the nearest pair of jeans and a tatty T-shirt, completing the outfit with a big comfy cardigan that you should really only ever wear when you are stopping in on your own. She found it hard to look her soon-to-be ex-husband in the eye.

'We've just come from the gym,' Dave had explained.

No shit, Sherlock, she'd thought as she'd looked at his outfit of shorts, T-shirt and bright white trainers. Debs had wondered how PFP didn't seem to have a bead of sweat on her, yet Dave looked like he'd been working in the garden all day, sweaty and red faced. How did he ever pull her? He was definitely punching way above his weight, although he looked as if he'd shifted a few pounds recently, even though his belly was still hanging over the top of his shorts.

'Come on, David darling, time to go,' PFP had trilled from the egg aisle. 'We've got to have an energy snack for lunch before we go to Zumba later. Bye, Deborah. Good to see you.'

Dave had muttered goodbye under his breath as he'd panted off down the aisle after her. Cheeky bitch, how dare she even speak to her.

Debs had gone over to the bakery section after that, eyeing up the cream cakes on display in the fridge – ninety-nine pence each or three for two pounds. It was a no brainer, she thought as she threw three into her basket. They'd do for pudding later. If she couldn't eat them all, she could have one for breakfast tomorrow.

As she'd walked along the clothing aisle, she'd picked up a pretty blue-and-yellow maxi dress that had caught her eye. She knew that most of her current clothes weren't going to fit her for the upcoming trip to Portugal and that it was probably better to go a size up, *again*, than spoil the holiday by being pissed off with herself because she couldn't fit into anything. It wasn't the normal sort of thing that she would wear but it was really pretty. She held it up against her body and looked in the mirror.

'Oh, my dear.' A little old lady who was walking past had stopped and put her hand on Debs' arm. 'That blue looks stunning on you. You *have* to buy it.'

Debs' had glowed and thanked the lady, and placed the dress in her trolley. It was amazing how a stranger could say something kind and make you feel a whole lot better. Kindness costs nothing and compliments really can lift someone's mood. Debs thought that the whole world would be a much nicer place if everyone would bear that in mind.

She was really looking forward to seeing the girls again. Well, they were hardly girls. Two of them were already fifty and two were about to be. It had been years since they'd seen each other for more than an evening, and she wondered what on earth they'd think of her when they saw how big she'd become. The last few times they'd been due to meet up, she'd cancelled last minute because she hadn't wanted them to see how she looked and couldn't bear to see the pity or sadness in their eyes. But she just needed to put on her big-girl pants, get it over and done with and not miss out again.

Chapter Four

'I'M REALLY NOT sure I should go, you know. I'm not sure it's the right thing to do.' Fiona's voice cracked, and she screwed up the tissue that she'd been holding onto.

She took her mum's hand and her mum smiled at her, content in her own little world, not really taking in anything that Fiona had said. Fiona wondered if her mum even knew who Fiona was at that particular moment.

'She'll be fine here with us, Fiona, and it's only for a week. Then Mum can come home with you again.' Brenda, the care home manager, was such a kind lady and Fiona totally trusted her. She really liked the home, and the room that they'd put aside for her mum, but she couldn't help but have mixed feelings.

'She'll be having a lovely little holiday herself and we'll have a lovely time together, won't we, Marion?'

'Can we do some singing? I like singing. I used

to play the piano, you know. Did you know I used to be a music teacher?'

'Did you, my love? Of course we can do some singing. We can do anything you want.'

Fiona smiled. As far as she knew her mother had never played the piano in her life and had never worked. She'd been a housewife, looking after her daughter until Fiona left home to go to university, and her husband Bill until he suffered a huge heart attack and passed away, leaving her bereft. At the time, Fiona had wanted to quit university and come home to her mother, but Marion had insisted that Bill would have wanted Fiona to continue her studies to make something of her life and go on to become a teacher. Perhaps that's what her mother was getting muddled about now.

Since Fiona had finally accepted what was happening to her mum, she had fought for a good while to get her mum's diagnosis confirmed so that they could get the help they needed. She'd had her suspicions for a long time but when she started to get calls from her mother's neighbours to say that she was walking down the street in her nightclothes, she knew something had to be done before it got any worse.

A ringing phone turned her into a nervous

wreck, having no idea what she was going to discover when she picked up.

It hadn't been easy. Numerous trips to the doctor, which were distressing enough for someone with Alzheimer's, then a visit to the memory clinic, had been the final step before they could all move forward.

Fiona had given up her job as a teacher, determined to look after her mum and spend as much time with her as possible. She'd immediately cleared out her mum's bungalow and she'd moved in with Fiona and at first it had been OK. Manageable even. But being around her mum every day made Fiona realise just how much and how quickly she had been deteriorating.

Fiona had taken her mum out for lunch recently with Samantha. Bearing in mind that they'd known each other all through childhood, when Marion asked Samantha who she was when she got in the car and then at the pub had asked her again, it hit Fiona hard that things were changing dramatically as well as quickly.

However, she'd learnt over the last few months, with the help of a brilliant support group, that it was no good getting frustrated with her mum because she didn't know what she was doing or saying. They helped her see the funny side of things where they could, too and that balanced the immense sadness she seemed to carry around with her most of the time.

When she'd met Brenda at a social group that they went to every Thursday night, she'd found her so easy to talk to and ended up pouring out her heart, telling her that she'd been invited to a fiftieth birthday celebration in Portugal but couldn't even consider it and didn't know how to tell her friends.

Brenda just happened to be the manager of Chase Lodge, a nursing home on the outskirts of Cannock Chase Forest, and just a couple of miles from Fiona's house. She handed Fiona her card and asked her to call her and have a look round. It was a beautiful place, full of happy staff who really seemed to enjoy looking after the residents, and in principle it sounded perfect, but now it was only a few days away, she was getting more and more nervous.

'It's just a week's respite for both you and Marion, my lovely. We're going to have a super time and so are you, so please, stop worrying. She's in good hands. And it'll do you *both* good. Her spending a few days, and the odd night, here before you go, should put both your minds at rest. She's quite familiar with the place now, and at least you can see that she's settled and happy here.'

She knew that Brenda was right but she felt so much guilt. Guilt that she was going to go off and enjoy herself. Guilt at leaving her mother behind. Guilt because as life evolves the child becomes the parent. And guilt at the fact that sometimes she wished it was all over.

As she walked away from the room, she swallowed down a lump that was forming in her throat and sincerely hoped that she was doing the right thing. She wondered whether she'd ever be able to forgive herself if anything happened to her mum while she was away. She clutched her chest as the thought occurred to her – what if this was the last time she ever saw her mum alive? A tear rolled down her cheek.

She glanced over her shoulder one more time and saw her mum turn to Brenda. In a very loud whisper, she heard her mum say, 'She's pretty. Who is that lady that just left?' She smiled a sad smile. Alzheimer's is a cruel disease, but you had to embrace it instead of fighting it to get through.

Chapter Five

'SO THERE ARE some meals in the freezer in case you are too busy to cook. You just need to remember to pull them out each morning to defrost. There's a list on the fridge to say which of the boys are doing what activities after school each day and what they should be doing at the weekend. And I've arranged for a cleaning company to come in on Monday morning to tidy up before I get back.' Olivia went over to kiss the boys, who were both looking a bit shell shocked. Had they thought that she wouldn't go through with her holiday?

Seb looked so sad. 'Do you have to go, Mum? Why can't we come with you?'

'Because I'm going with my friends and it's an adult holiday, darling. No kids allowed.' She tried a laugh, but felt a knot of guilt churn in her stomach. She had *never* been away without her family before, but she knew that it was something that she *really* needed. 'I'll be back before you know it.'

Her older son chipped in. 'Oh God, can you imagine going on holiday with Mum and her old crone friends? No thank you! I'd rather stay here and play on my Xbox.'

Olivia opened her mouth to say that James shouldn't be on it for more than a couple of hours a day, and then decided that George could parent as he saw fit. He wouldn't let any harm come to them; he just wouldn't do it the way that she did.

She walked over to where George was sitting watching the sports news on the TV and kissed him on his bald head. He turned away from her. He clearly still had the severe hump with her.

Hector, their tri-coloured English Setter, was curled up in his basket and when he saw her pick up her suede loafers from the shoe rack, cocked his ears and bounded over to her, thinking he was going out for a walk.

'Sorry, darling. But Steve from ChasinTails will be here to walk you in an hour. He'll be in every day till I'm back, so at least I know you'll have two decent walks every day and you won't be hassling this lot.' She ruffled the fur on Hector's head. She adored him. The whole family had cajoled her for months on end to have a dog. They all promised to look after it and take it for walks. The novelty wore off in less than a week, and none of them could understand why he loved her the most, even though she was the one who made sure he was fed, watered and walked every day. After first feeling that the responsibility of a dog was a burden, she'd ended up embracing being a doggy mum and realised that getting out of the house for a walk was a godsend and took her away from the stresses and strains of her needy family.

'Don't look so glum, Pembertons! I'll only be gone for a week. Love you all, bye-eee!'

She grabbed her sunhat, popped her latest designer shades on, which completed the summery outfit of three-quarter-length jeans and a floaty white linen shirt, and went out to grab her Uber, leaving her family behind. She'd rather hoped that George might drive her to the airport, but once she'd told him she was going away he'd been very cool with her and was now sulking so much that he had stopped talking to her completely. She hoped that this holiday would make them all appreciate her and help them stand on their own feet a little more.

Oh boy, she really needed this break.

Chapter Six

CRAMMING HER SMALL case shut, Samantha couldn't believe that everything had fitted in it. They were staying in a villa, so she hadn't packed too many dressy clothes, choosing instead cut-offs and vest tops, which she felt more comfortable in than anything. A couple of dresses for the evenings should see her through if they went anywhere nice. She felt too old for bikinis, so had opted for a couple of tummy-tucking swimming costumes. Not that she needed any assistance, as she was very proud of the fact that through careful eating and a great metabolism, she still had the same size-10 figure she'd had since she was a teenager.

While browsing the book aisle in her local supermarket, she had treated herself to half a dozen paperbacks to take away. Reading was her favourite pastime and she couldn't decide between quite a few, so she threw caution to the wind and bought them all. She liked an eclectic mix of genres from crime thrillers to romcoms – she loved a time-slip historical read too – and could while away hours between the pages of a novel. She smiled as she realised she hadn't left any books out for her hand luggage, so she'd nothing to read on the plane. Clearly she'd subconsciously wanted to browse the airport book store and pick up another one for the journey.

She hoisted the suitcase case off her bed, smoothing the cover, making sure it looked perfect for her return. One thing she always did before she went on holiday was to change the duvet cover and sheets, so she had a nice clean bed to come back to. The other thing she was quite habitual about was bleaching the loos! It was always the very last thing she did before she left. She and her brother used to roll their eyes when their mum insisted on doing these things when they were children, even before leaving for just a weekend away.

Recalling this memory made her smile. She'd give anything to chat to her mum one more time. They'd had such a close relationship and used to do everything together. She'd been an amazing grandmother to Peter, helping Samantha through some really tough times. Even though it had been thirteen years since she'd passed away after a ten-year battle with cancer, Samantha missed her every single day and her heart still ached to reach out and hug her.

The sound of a horn brought her back to the present, and she blew a kiss to the photograph of her mum, which was on the wall in the hallway. Just before Samantha opened the front door, she noticed the notebook sitting on the table at the bottom of the stairs and popped it in her handbag, then quickly fired off one last text. It was short and sweet.

Off to Portugal today, will keep in touch. Would love to hear from you when you have the chance x

She couldn't do any more than she was doing. The last nine months had been really tough. She hadn't realised quite how much she would miss him and she was incredibly lonely, not knowing what to do with herself. It was so hard to distance herself from that other life, but she had decided that she couldn't sit wallowing day after day, wondering if he'd ever text her back. She needed to make some major changes and shake up her life, and now she'd got used to the idea, she knew that the trip to Portugal would be just the job to kick-start her into action.

As the front door slammed behind her, she

looked up at her house and realised that when she saw it next she'd have a plan for the future and, hopefully, a great suntan.

Chapter Seven

THE LAST THING Debs wanted to do before she left for the airport was empty the fridge and put the bins out. God, she missed Dave more than ever when she had to put the bins out. That had always been his job. Along with cutting the lawns and cleaning the cars. But, she reminded herself, he had also always been a bit of a lazy one, and didn't do a fat lot else around the house, so she wasn't *that* much worse off being on her own.

However, she missed him terribly in the evenings. They were the worst times for her. She was dreading the approaching autumn months, when the dark descended earlier and earlier, and curtains were shut and you felt barricaded in your house and it was as if you should really be going to bed at eight p.m. She had underestimated the complete and utter loneliness she'd feel once he left, and the silence in the house. It was really time to do something about it.

What she didn't miss was picking up his dirty

boxers from the bedroom floor and wet towels from the bathroom tiles. *And* finding toenail clippings on the toilet seat. She shuddered at the memory.

She was still furious with him from when she came home early from work one day last week to find him sitting on the lounge floor, watching TV. Cheeky bastard. He'd had the audacity to ask her what she was doing home at that time of the day. When she asked him what he was doing there, and reminded him that he didn't live there any more, he said that he preferred this house because Penny was always cleaning everything away and he couldn't relax there as much. He'd also put some washing in the machine, as he knew how to work Debs' one better than the one at Penny's house. What a shame he hadn't seemed to know how it worked when he lived there. Debs had told him in no uncertain terms that if he didn't shift his backside immediately, she'd be straight round to Penny's house to tell her and she could see the horror on his face at the thought that PFP might find out.

She opened to fridge to see if anything needed binning. The last thing she wanted was to come back to stinky old milk and mouldy bread. While she threw things away, she noticed a chocolate bar that she'd hidden from herself at the back of the fridge and scoffed it. When she returned, she was going to stock her fridge with healthy stuff only and it was going to be the start of her new regime. She was determined this time to lose this weight once and for all.

Dragging the bins up the passageway at the side of the house, she cursed Dave's workmanship when, in her haste, she snagged a nail opening the back gate, which was practically falling apart. He'd tried to repair it, but he wasn't the best at handiwork, yet also refused to pay anyone to do it. Their house was therefore in need of a lot of tender loving care. She deserved to live in a nice home, she decided, so she was going to save up and get things done. Or she could even move house. She didn't feel the same about this one now, anyway, and didn't particularly want to see her ex-husband and his new girlfriend flaunting their life in front of her. Perhaps it was time to move on.

Grabbing a nail file from a bowl on the kitchen worktop, she smoothed the nail until it looked as good as new. Walking past the hall mirror, she caught sight of herself and cringed. She was wearing a floaty flowery top over grey linen trousers and she looked huge. She'd stopped looking in mirrors years ago when Dave started making fun of her and her weight. He hadn't realised how hurtful his comments were and the more he taunted her, the more depressed she became and the more she ate.

She hoped the clothes she'd chosen carefully to pack were appropriate for this holiday. She wore black trousers and a logoed T-shirt for her job at the children's nursery. All the staff wore the same, so she didn't really have to think about clothes too much. She hadn't seen the girls for such a long time, and hadn't a clue what their plans were for the time they were away, and didn't want to make a fool of herself looking like mutton dressed up as lamb. She just hoped that everything still fitted her. She really should have tried it all on. She'd not worn some of the stuff since their disastrous holiday in Benidorm last summer when the problems in hers and Dave's relationship really started to shine through. That was when she started to have her suspicions about Dave as he kept disappearing, and she'd caught him a couple of times chatting quietly into his phone and then making out that it was someone from work. She should have trusted her instincts back then.

Oh well, it was all water under the bridge now. She couldn't change anything that had already happened, all she could influence was the future, she thought as the taxi beeped its horn. She grabbed a flapjack from the side cupboard and shoved it in her handbag in case she needed a snack on the way. The driver came in and took the medium-sized black case from the hallway. As she shut the front door, she took a big breath and wondered how she'd feel on her return and what the future held.

Chapter Eight

'JUST CHECK AGAIN, please, that you've got my number, Brenda? You will call if there's a problem, won't you? I'll just pop back into her room and say goodbye. *Again.*'

Brenda smiled at Fiona sympathetically and stroked her arm. 'She'll be absolutely fine. You should just go, Fiona. She'll be perfectly happy here with us. I'll look after her like she's my own mother. You have my word.'

'Thank you, and I know you will, but I'll just pop in one more time.'

Fiona popped her head around the door of her mother's room. Sunlight flooded through the large bay window onto the chintzy wallpaper and the various photographs of her mum with her family which sat on top of the pine dressing table. It was a lovely room, just across from the main lounge, where Marion could go if she wanted to spend her time with others. Now she was sitting in a wing-backed armchair in the corner of the room, with her feet on a footstool. A blanket lay across her knees and she was propped up on big squishy cushions. She looked really comfy while she was watching *Homes Under the Hammer* on the TV.

'Hello, dear, are you one of the nurses?' Her mum smiled sweetly. 'Have you brought me some lunch?'

'No, Mum, it's me, Fiona. Your daughter. You're here because I'm going away for a few days. Do you remember? You've only just had your breakfast. Porridge and honey. It's not time for lunch yet.'

'Daughter? I have a daughter? Well, I never. When and how on earth did that happen?' Her mum looked at her, puzzled.

Strange how she focussed on just one part of a conversation, Fiona thought.

'Go! Just go,' Brenda laughed as she shooed her away. 'She'll be fine, I promise. Have a great break.'

'Bye, Mum, see you soon.'

Her mum reached up to her, and stroked her face, tucking a stray tendril of wavy brown hair behind her daughter's ear.

'Goodbye, my darling. See you tonight.' She'd already forgotten that Fiona was going away, but as Fiona looked deep into her mum's eyes, before kissing her on the forehead, she swore that she saw a hint of recognition.

Sometimes there was a light in her mum's eyes and a glimmer of hope came to Fiona that her mum was back, but it lasted mere seconds, before Marion became confused again. It was desperately upsetting to see her in this way. However, it was something that they had to deal with in the best way for everyone.

Fiona had been so distressed at first when her mum didn't recognise her; now it just made her feel sad. It wasn't her mum's fault. It was her brain playing tricks. And she knew that it was only going to get worse. Dementia affected everyone in a family in so many ways. Fiona's mind was permanently in turmoil and she carried a permanent ache in her chest. She knew she needed to do some serious thinking. She was so grateful that she had met Brenda, who had been a wonderful shoulder to cry on when she needed a friend who totally understood.

Fiona grabbed her handbag and, as she headed through the entrance doors, a big fat tear rolled down her cheek. Clutching her chest as she walked away, she felt so emotional at leaving her mum here, but knew it was the best thing for both of them right now. She'd never needed a break more and she would use this holiday to get her head round things before they got even worse.

She wasn't quite sure how she made it from the care home to the airport car park, through the tears, but pulled herself together once she'd parked, then made her way to the terminal building. She needed a gin.

Chapter Nine

OLIVIA WAS THE first of the party due to arrive into Faro airport. As the plane came in to land, and the captain announced, 'Cabin crew, five minutes to landing,' on its descent over the rugged coast line and beautiful long stretches of golden sand, she could see sail boats bobbing on the water and her heart gave a little skip of excitement. It was a glorious day, the sky a vivid cobalt blue and the heat of the morning hit her as soon as the cabin doors opened, along with fuel fumes, and as she stood at the top of the steps, she held her face to the sun and sighed.

All the flights were due to land within an hour of each other. Fiona chose to fly in from Doncaster because she could get the cheapest flight, Samantha from Luton for similar reasons, Debs from East Midlands as it was her nearest and as Olivia preferred to fly British Airways instead of cheap and cheerful, she was flying out of Birmingham.

The plan was to meet at the airport where the

fabulous Mikey, who she'd arranged everything with, had promised there would be transport to the villa.

Mikey was such a find. She'd just told him what she wanted and he did all the work – it was a perfect pairing.

As soon as she'd made it to the baggage area, Olivia immediately headed to the ladies' toilets. She touched up her make-up to help her look a little less sweaty, spritzed herself with Chanel No. 5 and popped her Carolina Herrera sunglasses on her head while she waited for her Louis Vuitton cases to catch up with her. Once she'd retrieved them from the luggage carousel, she pulled her trolley to one side and swapped her flat loafers for some strappy wedges, which were just inside her case. Then she headed for the nearest coffee shop, where she grabbed an anti-bac wipe from her Mulberry handbag, cleared the table of coffee slops and crumbs, and then sat scrolling through her phone until a tap on her shoulder startled her.

Debs squealed in delight to see her, held her at arm's length and said, 'Look at you. Mrs Glamorous! God! You look amazing, Liv!'

Olivia had forgotten that she'd been called Liv. George *always* called her Olivia and, obviously, she was called Mum most of the time, or Sebastian's mum, James's mum or George's wife. 'Liv' seemed to be a person who existed years ago and she hoped very much that Liv was still alive and kicking and would be very much on this holiday with her girls.

'And you! Let me look at you! You look fabulous, Debs. So well.'

'You mean fat! I'm not daft! I know I'm fat, Liv.' She laughed to hide the emotion she was feeling.

'Well, there's certainly a little more of you since the last time I saw you, Debs, but that must have been over fifteen years ago. You still look gorgeous, darling. You always do.' She kissed her friend on both cheeks. When in Europe and all that.

'Woohoo! Over here!' They looked towards a waving Fiona and ran over to her, squishing her in a huge hug. Olivia stamped her feet like a dog full of joy to see its owner. She was so happy to see her pals. She hadn't realised just how much she'd missed them.

'I do hope you're not having a group hug without me,' a voice shouted across the concourse, and Samantha rushed across, dropping her bags to join in.

There was much squealing all around. Travellers passing by smiled and laughed along at the teenage behaviour of these middle-aged ladies who were showing such joy at their reunion.

'OMG! It is sooo good to see you ladies. I'd forgotten how much I loved our group hugs!' Olivia clung to her friends for dear life. She was quite chilled after a miniature bottle of Bollinger on the flight, even though it had been early. She was glad to be free of her family shackles for the next few days and was so looking forward to catching up with these dearest of friends that she used to know so well, and finding out how the last few years had treated them all.

A deep, sexy voice sounded from nowhere. 'Now, if I'm not mistaken, you gorgeous four must be the Pemberton party. I'm Mikey, and I'm all yours for the duration of your time here in Portugal.'

Four sets of eyes lit up at the sight of this dashingly handsome, tall, slim young man stood in front of them and lots of air kissing went on for a minute or two before a passer-by shouted, 'Get a room!'

They all roared with laughter as Mikey broke free, loaded all of the cases onto a trolley and led the ladies out to the front of the arrivals hall where the brilliant sunshine dazzled them all, until they grabbed their sunglasses. To their delighted surprise, a long black limo awaited them. Mikey introduced them all to Vicente, the driver, who nodded at them in acknowledgement and put the cases in the boot. Mikey then joined them in the back and poured them all a glass of chilled prosecco, even though Samantha said that it was only late morning.

Debs giggled. 'It's always six o'clock somewhere in the world, darling! Cheers!' This had been their standard saying when they were out and about in their younger years.

They all clinked glasses and shouted 'yamas', another tradition from their Greek holiday years ago, as they began their short journey to their destination, which was just outside the marina resort of Vilamoura.

At the end of a small tree-lined cul-de-sac, a stunning, huge, whitewashed villa with a terracotta-tiled roof stood out against the bright-blue sky. There was a collective gasp as they all saw where they would be staying and realised that it was somewhere very special. White stone lions guarded the pillars either side of black cast-iron gates, and a tiled terracotta walkway led through a small but beautifully manicured front garden – filled with lush greenery and magnificent magenta and amethyst blooms on the most glorious bougainvillea shrubs – up to an arched wooden front door. Mikey winked at Olivia and she discreetly nodded at him in acknowledgement. He'd done her proud.

Mikey helped them all out of the limo – not the easiest of cars to exit gracefully – and led them to the front door, bowing as he invited them to enter, while the driver started to pull the cases from the boot.

'OMG! This entrance hall is probably bigger than the whole of my downstairs! And oh my, look at that gorgeous fountain in the middle!' Debs exclaimed at the centrepiece in the bright, airy reception room and the sweeping tiled staircase on the right that led to a huge balcony landing with a large picture window. 'Although that trickling water is making me need a wee.'

'Wow! I could just see myself swishing across that landing and sweeping down that staircase in a beautiful ballgown!' Fiona couldn't believe her eyes. 'I can't believe this has only cost us five hundred pounds for five days. What a bargain!'

Mikey and Olivia exchanged a sneaky glance, which Samantha clocked and raised her eyebrows thinking that maybe Olivia hadn't quite told the entire truth about the cost of the villa. She must remember to talk to her about it later.

Debs wandered through the doorway on the left and yelled, 'OMG! Look at this view!'

The others joined her, their heels clicking on the white tiled floors and each of them gasped a sharp intake of breath as they saw the elegant yet simply furnished lounge area, with leather sofas and marble-topped coffee table, where the light colours added to the overall feeling of space. Bi-fold doors at the end of the room opened onto a huge terraced area decked out with rattan sunbeds and lounging sofas, and the most stunning infinity pool with a bubbling jacuzzi area in the near corner. It all overlooked the rugged coastline and the sparkling turquoise waters of the Atlantic Ocean beyond.

'Ladies, when you've finished admiring that splendid view, let me show you more. Over here, you have the kitchen to the right. There's a welcome pack of essentials that should see you through until you get the chance to make a shopping list. Cooked meats, a variety of cheeses, breads and salad, as I thought you might be ready for lunch. And I've popped a couple of bottles of white wine in the fridge and there's some red on the countertop by the cooker. There's ice in the freezer and, at Olivia's request, plenty of tonic and a bottle of Bombay Sapphire for those of you who might like a G and T.

'And then for your meal this evening, I have a chef coming to do a barbecue. I've got a selection of meat, fish and salad. I do hope that's OK for you. I just thought that after a morning of travelling, after lunch you might be ready for a nice relaxing afternoon by the pool. But if you'd rather go out for a meal, I can swap things around or cancel the barbecue completely. Oh, and before I forget to tell you, the number for Vicente is on the side of the fridge. Just call him any time you need him and he'll take you anywhere you want to go.'

'Liv, you really have thought of everything. Thank you so much for organising it all. You really are amazing.'

'You are so welcome, Fiona! I wouldn't say I've thought of everything but I've certainly thought of the essentials. And it's Mikey who's done all the hard work. I just told him what I thought we would all want. I certainly want to get a break from driving and cooking while I'm away and Mikey suggested a driver on standby, rather than being flung around in the back of a taxi. Is everyone OK with staying in this afternoon and then we can maybe go and have a wander around either later today or in the morning?'

There were nods all round. Samantha was still

speechless from the view and couldn't tear her eyes away, still not convinced this place had really cost five hundred pounds to hire.

'Right then! Let's go check out the bedrooms. Bagsy the biggest!' Olivia headed for the stairs.

'Some things never change!' Samantha smirked and there were giggles all round.

'And that's something you definitely don't have to worry about because the bedrooms are all pretty much the same size and every one of them is en suite, so no sharing of bathrooms required. I know that's something important to you ladies.'

'God, Mikey, are you married? You'd make the most wonderful husband. And if you're not will you marry me, please?' Debs roared with laughter.

Mikey grinned. 'I'm not, but ask me again tomorrow and I might say yes! Come on, ladies, let's get you upstairs.'

Debs guffawed. 'It's been a long time since a man said that to me, Mikey! You'd better be careful!'

He laughed as he led the way. 'Ooh, you big tease. So, ladies, there are six bedrooms in the villa. Four at the back that overlook the sea, and two at the front that overlook the gardens and many tall trees laden with lemons and limes.'

They chose their rooms pretty quickly. Each

room was, like the rest of the villa, simply furnished yet stunningly beautiful, with cool tiled floors and French doors which led onto a furnished private terrace that overlooked the shimmering sea.

'I think I might just sit and watch the sea for the whole time we are here!' Olivia laughed and then said, 'Listen.' There was complete silence. 'No kids, no husbands, just peace and quiet! And you beautiful lot! I am *so* looking forward to spending time with you guys and getting to know you all over again.'

The driver must have been operating in stealth mode as he somehow managed to get their cases onto the gallery landing without anyone even noticing, so they agreed to meet downstairs in half an hour for a long and relaxing lunch after they'd unpacked.

'Ladies, I'll leave you to get sorted. If you need me, my number is by the phone in the hallway. There's a map there too, so you know where the nearest shops, bars and restaurants are. If you need anything, your wish is my command. I can pretty much arrange anything. And I do like a challenge.'

Mikey winked at them, bowed and backed away, then skittered down the stairs to the waiting limo, which drove off down the lane.

MIKEY TUCKED HIS hair behind his ear as he spoke on the phone. 'OK, Mum, that's fine. See you soon.'

Mikey tried hard to be chirpy on the phone but was dreading his parents arriving tomorrow and that, at some point during their stay, they'd find out the truth. He'd put them into the villa next door to the Pemberton party. One of the perks of being the best sales person in the company was getting a whopping discount for family members and he knew that his mum would love the villa. That might distract them enough so that they wouldn't notice the changes in his life since the last time they saw him.

Chapter Ten

DEBS HAD ALREADY made a start on lunch when Olivia arrived downstairs. She'd set the table, put out the cold meats and was preparing a salad. 'Glass of wine, Liv?'

'Oh, not for me thanks, love. I'll have some sparkling water if there is some. Don't want to get drunk and end up needing to go to sleep and wasting an afternoon that I can be topping up my tan around that amazing pool.'

Debs realised that what Olivia called 'wasting an afternoon' was exactly how she was planning to spend hers. When Liv wasn't looking, Debs looked her up and down. She had a beautiful figure, slim but with curves in all the right places, and was wearing a floral sarong over the top of a plain black swimming costume. Her boobs were amazing and Debs couldn't stop staring at her. She was so classy.

Liv still managed to look glamorous even when she was going to be sunbathing and there was a part of Debs that was dead jealous. She could never look like Liv. She was fat and frumpy and what she had thought was a glamorous sparkly kaftan at home seemed like a saggy old tent compared to that lovely outfit Liv was wearing. There was no bloody way she was getting her body out though, unless she was drunk, she knew that much. She topped up her glass of red wine, and Liv looked over and raised an eyebrow, noticing that she'd obviously already drunk one.

'Right, what do you want me to do then?' Liv asked.

'The rest of the food just needs putting on the table, everything is prepared. There's really nothing much to do at all. Mikey seems to have thought of everything to make our time here so easy. He really is a darling.'

'Oh, isn't he just? I'm so glad I found him. Shall we eat on the terrace then? May as well make the most of this gorgeous weather and that amazing sea view. We can sit inside at home.'

'Oh, now that sounds wonderful. Shall we start to take stuff outside?' Fiona asked, appearing in a strapless sundress and a big straw hat.

'Let me help too,' Samantha said, grabbing some bowls as she walked through the kitchen.

Debs' eyes roamed over her body too, and she

decided that Samantha was way too skinny and looked quite scruffy in a pair of cut-off denim shorts and a tatty old T-shirt. Samantha had always been a bit of a hippy chick in her younger years and her style hadn't really changed.

Debs reminded herself that they were all entitled to wear what they liked. They were on holiday, after all, and who was she to judge anyone else?

'Come on, you gorgeous, lot,' she called. 'Lunch is served!'

'GOD, I'M STUFFED,' Debs said as she popped yet another sweet baby pepper stuffed with cream cheese in her mouth and started to clear away. Fiona got up to help her.

'Oh, me too! That was lush! I've eaten more carbs in one meal than I ate last month. That bread was amazing. I might have to get up and go for a run in the morning.' Liv stretched and yawned. 'I can't believe I'm tired. I've done nothing so far today.'

'That's the trouble sometimes. You run around like a loon at home, and then you come away and stop. It's your body's way of telling you that you need to rest. From what you said over lunch, it sounds like you never stop running around after your family, Liv.' Samantha moved her chair nearer to Liv and into the line of the sun.

'Well, I don't, but it's not like I'm working like most people, is it? I shouldn't complain. But sometimes the constant neediness of my family is totally exhausting. It's my own fault though. It's the way I've made them. It's like I've created a monster family who can't do anything for themselves.'

She looked sad and Samantha started to wonder whether what people saw on the outside as the perfect family actually had more cracks than they might think possible.

'You're happy though, aren't you?' she asked.

Liv hesitated for just a little longer than Samantha expected her to before she answered, and Samantha realised that she'd hit a nerve. As she looked over at Liv she noticed a tear trickle down her cheek. Liv wiped it off and Samantha looked away discreetly.

'I'm fine, Sam, I just need a break. I'm shattered with it all. You guys and this place will energise me to get stuck right back in when I get home.'

'Perhaps you could try to make them a little more self-sufficient, Liv.'

'Ha! Seb is so lazy and dependent on me that he won't even wipe his own backside. James just grunts from morning to night and gives me attitude, and George treats me like a skivvy most of the time. And I'm so bloody stupid that I let him. I think the only one who really loves me is the dog.'

'You are far from stupid, Liv. You were cleverer than any of us when we were at uni, without even trying very hard. Perhaps you just need to have a think while you are here about making a few changes at home. The perfect time to think about stuff like that is when you're away from it all. To be honest, I think I'll be filling my notebook with lots of thoughts and making a big to-do list while I'm here.'

'So, what about you then, Sam? What's happening in your life?'

'Nothing, Liv. Nothing at all. That's the problem.'

'Oh well, we need to sort that out too then, don't we? I think this holiday is going to do us all some good.' Liv reached out and squeezed Samantha's hand. making Samantha realise that she really missed touch in her life. She had always been a tactile person. 'So, as you brought a notebook with you, does that mean that you're still a stationery addict?' asked Liv.

Samantha smiled as she remembered the delivery she'd had the day before from a stationery store. Notebooks, list pads, journals. She loved it all. 'You could say that.'

'More wine, anyone?' Debs came out brandishing another bottle of red. Samantha and Liv glanced knowingly at each other and Debs pretended that she didn't notice.

'Not for me, thanks. I want to appreciate this gorgeous weather.' Liv stood and stretched and made her way over to the rattan sunbeds. She sat down and sank into the padded cushions and sighed. She took off her kaftan and picked up her bottle of suntan lotion and slathered it over her body, while Debs stared at her amazing figure. How could she possibly still look that fabulous when she had just gone fifty?

'Me neither, thanks,' said Samantha. 'I'm going to grab my novel from my handbag and have a little read on that bed next to you, Liv, if you don't mind.'

'Fill your boots, Sam. I'm just going to lie here and be. Just be me. Without anyone needing me.'

'Well, don't mind if I do.' Debs grinned as she filled up her glass to the brim for the fourth time.

'You need to put some suntan lotion on, Debs,

or you'll burn.' Liv threw her a bottle of factor 40 and Debs put it down by the side of her bed. 'Yep, in a bit.'

Liv laughed. 'God, I need to remember that you are all adults and not one of my useless bloody family. If I didn't tell them what to do from morning to night they'd never even get out of bed, let alone dressed. I wonder if they all got off to school and work OK today.'

'I'm sure you'd have heard if they hadn't,' Debs replied from under her baseball cap.

'Well, if I hadn't turned my phone off the minute I arrived, I might have done,' Liv replied.

'Good for you, honey, good for you! I'm sure they'll cope one way or another,' Samantha said.

'Where's Fi?' Liv asked.

'Gone upstairs to make a phone call apparently. Not sure who to. All very mysterious if you ask me,' Debs replied as she picked up her glass of wine and downed the lot.

Two minutes later, she was snoring away.

'HONESTLY, FIONA, SHE'S absolutely fine. We've had a singer in this afternoon and she really enjoyed that. She loves a sing-song and even got up to have a dance at one point. We've had a singer in called Maddy Young. Lovely girl. Got all the old ones up dancing and singing. We've had a wonderful afternoon. Apparently she does gigs like this with her friend Beth in local care homes. They run a doggy day-care centre together too.'

'Oh, that's so good to hear, Brenda. I can't thank you enough. I really can't.'

'She's settled in so well, Fiona. She's absolutely fine, I promise you. Now go and relax with your friends. And I mean it when I say ring anytime you like to put your mind at rest, but go and have some fun and chill out.'

'Thank you, Brenda.'

As Fiona ended the call, she really believed Brenda was an angel on earth and just what she and Marion needed right now.

FIONA JOINED THE others on the terrace, and after they'd all either had a read or a snooze, peeled off her shorts and T-shirt to reveal her bright-red cossie.

'Last one in the pool is a loser!' she yelled as she gracefully dived in and emerged gasping for breath, for as soon as she hit the water she realised the pool wasn't heated.

'Fuck, that's cold!' she squealed. The others laughed and Debs woke up with a start.

'You coming in, Debs?' Fiona yelled at her.

'God, I need to wake up first. Anyone fancy a coffee?'

There were oohs and aahs all round and Debs went into the kitchen to try to work out how to use the silver contraption that Mikey had pointed out as being the coffee machine. As she opened and shut cupboards trying to find cups and the instructions for the coffee machine, she mumbled under her breath, 'What's wrong with bloody instant anyway? You need a degree to work this bloody thing!'

While she totally loved coffee, and needed it to get through each day, going into a coffee shop now, and queuing up for a latte or a cappuccino, took valuable minutes from her day. She wasn't the most patient of people and always found herself drumming her fingers on the countertop or scrolling through her phone before she got annoyed with the waiting.

Finally finding the instructions, she fathomed out how to make four coffees, which according to the machine were meant to be lattes but she wasn't really sure. She hoped they tasted better than they looked. There was clearly an art to posh coffee making.

Placing the tray on the table, along with a plate

of Portuguese tarts she had found in the fridge, she sat back down on her sunbed carefully. She was always scared to death that one of those things would break under her weight.

Fiona yelled, 'Thanks, Debs. Come in and join us. It's lovely and refreshing once you get over the initial shock.' Liv and Samantha laughed and nodded in agreement.

'I'll come in later. I'm just going to sit and catch up on Facebook,' she said as she thought that there was no way she was getting her dress off and letting people see her body. No bloody way at all.

Chapter Eleven

FIONA ROSE FROM the pool and draped a robe around her shoulders to keep her warm and dry. 'Right, I'm off to get my book from upstairs. I bought the book that was number one in the charts at the airport bookshop. Hope it's a good one. Can't wait to try to get back into reading this week.'

'Oh, I've brought tons of books with me if you run out, Fi.' Samantha smiled. They had easily slipped back into the names they'd called each other when they were younger.

Debs got up and said she was popping to the loo before she got comfy again and asked if anyone wanted anything. They all shook their heads and realised that they were all quite content just as they were at the moment.

Liv grabbed the stripy beach towel from her sunbed and dried herself. Once again, Debs looked at her from under her sunglasses as she walked past, hoping that she couldn't see her staring. How on earth can she look that fantastic at her age? Her stomach was flat, her boobs looked as magnificently perky as those of an eighteen-year-old, and she still managed to look stunning when she'd come out of a pool whereas Debs would have looked like a complete fright.

'You're still as gorgeous as you were when you were younger, you know, Liv. I don't know how you do it.'

Liv lay down on her sunbed gracefully. Debs noticed such a difference from when she had done it. She couldn't work out if the creaking noises were coming from her body or the sunbed. And she seemed to have to make ooh and aah noises as she raised herself and headed off into the kitchen.

'If you don't mind me asking, how come your boobs don't disappear under your armpits like mine do when I lie down?' Samantha laughed as she looked down at her own chest.

Liv looked over and winked at her. 'Mmmm! Let's just say it was more natural in the old days, shall we?'

Samantha raised an eyebrow and decided she would try to find out over the course of the holiday. She wondered if Liv had had a boob job or something. She was dying to know, although it didn't really matter anyway. She looked fabulous no matter what.

'God, I adore the sun,' Liv muttered. 'I can literally feel it recharging my body and my soul. Or that might just be that I've not got two children fighting around me. I can't remember the last time I lay around a pool like this and just had peace and quiet. It's gorgeous. I don't even want to read. I just want to lie here and appreciate it. I'm so glad you all agreed to come.'

'Well, you did get a bargain price after all, didn't you, Liv?' Samantha said questioningly.

Liv poked her tongue into her cheek. 'Yes, it was such a great deal. Lucky, weren't we?'

'You can't fool me, Liv. There's no bloody way that you got this for the money that you told us. What's really going on?'

'Oh, please don't say anything to the others. I've just become accustomed to luxury and, after all, when you go away, you should have somewhere better than where you live. Otherwise, what's the point of going away? You may as well have stayed at home.' She gave a high-pitched laugh. 'George told me to spend what I wanted to, and I know that you guys wouldn't have let me pay for the whole thing, so I thought that five hundred pounds sounded reasonable.'

'Reasonable? It's amazing. But I feel really

guilty that you've paid for the majority of it. Can we maybe give you some more towards it?'

'Honestly, no. It's fine, but thank you so much for offering. George just had a big windfall, so gave me half. He's very generous with his money. This is my gift to you guys. We all deserve a little treat from time to time. It's just a shame that George can't give up his time as easily as he gives up his money.'

Her voice sounded wobbly and once again Samantha wondered whether Liv was experiencing serious problems in her marriage. She hoped that it was just a blip and that coming away would make her miss her family and become eager to get back. Liv touched her Tiffany necklace. Samantha had noticed her do this a few times, perhaps it was a comfort thing.

'Don't worry about me, Sam. Honestly.' She drew her knees in close to her chest. 'I just need to make a few changes. Then I'll be fine.'

Debs and Fiona walked back onto the terrace at the same time but from different directions. There were doors galore in this place. Debs realised that she'd probably have to check them all every night more than once before she could settle into bed. Since she'd lived alone, it was something that she found herself doing obsessively, even though she hadn't opened some of them for weeks.

'I'm looking forward to the barbecue tonight. Although after that huge lunch, I'm not sure I'll need anything else.' She giggled as she popped a Portuguese tart in her mouth. 'What does everyone fancy doing while we're out here? Anything in particular?'

'Well, I've been doing a bit of reading about the area.' Samantha thought she may as well mention what she'd discovered through her many evenings of internet research.

The other girls all exchanged glances and grinned.

'What?' Samantha questioned.

'You always were the swotty one who looked into everything. We knew you would, so we left all the research all up to you! Remember when we were in Corfu for our twenty-first birthday celebrations and we were all happy to go with the flow, but you had an itinerary for us?' Fiona asked. They all giggled as memories of the holiday they'd had to celebrate the year of their twenty-first birthdays came flooding back, all thinking how very grateful they were that their friendship was still going twenty-nine years later.

'You are awesome, Samantha. Saves the rest of us doing the groundwork.' Fiona sniggered.

'Well, there's no point in going away and wasting time, so I wanted to check out what was in the area. I know I'm always the *sensible* one, but it's a good job one of us is.'

They all laughed again good-heartedly and Samantha continued. 'I'd love to go into the marina one of the days or evenings. It looks gorgeous and there are some beautiful restaurants overlooking all the yachts that are moored up. And there's a casino too. Perhaps we should try our luck one night.'

'Ooh, that's a fabulous idea. I've never been to a casino.' Debs grinned widely and her eyes sparkled.

'I'd love to have a go at playing golf. Perhaps Mikey could arrange lessons for us, if anyone else fancies it. George plays all the time and maybe he'd notice me a bit more if I could play golf.' Liv tittered for what seemed longer than necessary, then went quiet and stared into space.

'I'm up for anything and everything,' Samantha announced. 'This is the new me from now on!'

'Right, well, it's four o'clock and we apparently have a chef coming in at seven to start cooking dinner. I don't know about you guys, but I'm going to make the most of being out in this lovely sunshine and my family being in a different country, and have a snooze. So you can all shut up talking now, thank you very much.' Liv laughed.

'Oh, how rude.' Samantha laughed back. 'Bloody good idea, though. I'm going to have a read.'

A grunt came from the sunbed on the end of the row, and Debs was fast asleep, snoring her head off. Fiona stood and moved one of the sunshades above her. She'd noticed her friend was already going a bit pink. Despite Liv mentioning suntan lotion earlier, Debs hadn't taken any notice.

'I'm going to go up to my room and call the home again, just to make sure Mum's OK, then have a proper sleep in my bed. It looks so comfy. Shall we meet down here around six thirty for pre-dinner drinks?' Fiona suggested.

'Mmmm!' Liv and Samantha mumbled in unison.

Debs farted loudly in her sleep and they all giggled like schoolgirls. Laughter with your friends is one of the best things you can ever have in life, Liv thought to herself as she drifted off to sleep. And it had been missing from her life for a long time.

'LADIES, MY NAME is Josep and I am at your service for this evening.'

Debs raised her eyebrows and muttered, 'Yum! He could definitely service me.'

Samantha dug her in the ribs to shut her up.

The chef ignored their tittering and continued. 'I have prepared these cocktails for you.'

He handed sugar-rimmed glasses to them all and received a chorus of oohs and aahs as the delicious gin-based drink hit the spot. 'And now I will go into the barbecue area and your dinner will be served on the terrace in one hour.'

'God, I think I've died and gone to heaven,' Debs announced. 'A man who makes you cocktails *and* cooks. Do you know, in eighteen years of being married to Dave, he only once cooked me a meal, and that was something he chucked in the microwave then waited for a ping.'

'I'm the same, Debs,' said Liv. 'I don't think George has even done that. He got his mother over when Seb and James were born, so he didn't have to do anything even then. It's her fault that he's the way he is. If she hadn't pandered to his every whim as a child, he'd be a bit more self-sufficient now. The trouble is, my sons are the same. I really need to do something about that before it's too late and some poor unsuspecting woman has to live a life of slavery to either of them.' Liv looked so sad and serious, but decided she was giving too much away and tried to lighten the mood. 'It's a good job Josep's mother didn't pander to him. He seems very capable, eh, Debs?'

'He's gorgeous. Did you see his backside? Phwoar. After Dave left, I never thought I'd want another man, but Josep has definitely stirred my loins.'

They all laughed. Debs had always been the funniest in the group. The one who said out loud what everyone else was thinking – which had got her into trouble many a time. Liv wished she was more like Debs and that she wasn't so serious all the time. Perhaps she needed to be more relaxed.

'OMG, Debs, remember what happened on the beach in Corfu?'

The girls all cackled loudly, and Debs flushed bright red, remembering the events of a holiday when they were in their late teens. Debs had met a handsome Greek guy called Tomaso, who had been down at the beach with a couple of his friends. Liv and Debs were in the sea, and Fiona and Samantha had stayed on the beach. Debs clearly hadn't realised at the time how much her voice was carrying.

'God, Liv, have you seen the body on Tomaso? Oh, I could smother cold Greek yoghurt all over those abs and lick it right off. He's bloody gorgeous. That body!'

Fiona and Samantha had started coughing in an attempt to cover for her, but it hadn't worked. When Liv and Debs got back to the beach, Tomaso offered to go and fetch some ice creams. He then winked at Debs and asked her if she wanted some Greek yoghurt instead. Debs had flushed bright red and wanted the ground to open up and swallow her. Luckily everyone had found it funny and it was one of the many things from that fabulous holiday that was always mentioned when they'd met up over the years.

It was the promise that they'd made to each on that holiday, that had brought them to Portugal. A promise made, as they sat on the beach one morning after a night out, watching the sun rise above the ocean, when they held hands and vowed to be together when they celebrated their fiftieth birthdays too, even though in those days, their fiftieth birthdays had seemed like a lifetime away.

Time seemed to fly by so quickly as they sat on the sofas on the terrace chatting easily; laughing and reminiscing over that holiday while the aroma of sweet wood smoke mixed with garlic wafted over from time to time.

A subtle cough drew their attention to Josep, who informed them that dinner was served. As they approached the outside dining areas, Fiona gasped out loud. Modern lanterns flickered all around the terrace and pool area and fairy lights covered the canopy under which the huge marble table was laden with a mountain of food. A paella pan full to the brim with rainbow rice and giant prawns sat as the centrepiece, with mouth-watering mussels resting against the outside rim of the metal pan. Steam rose from a plate of traditional Piri Piri chicken and vegetable skewers adorned another platter. A chopping board was overflowing with a variety of cheeses and crusty bread.

Debs smacked her lips together, practically salivating at the food. 'This looks absolutely delicious, Josep. Thank you so much.'

'A magnificent feast for magnificent ladies. Let me get you some wine.'

Liv winked at the others as he filled their glasses.

'How on earth did we get all this for five hundred pounds, Liv?' Fiona asked.

Samantha and Liv exchanged furtive glances.

'Well, George did make a generous donation towards keeping his wife and her friends happy,' Liv admitted. Her friends smiled.

The four women raised their glasses.

'Cheers, George.'

Chapter Twelve

SUNLIGHT STREAMED THROUGH the bi-fold doors as the clattering of cups woke Debs. Through half-closed eyes, she could see that Liv was creeping around in the kitchen, trying to make as little noise as possible while she made coffee. Debs felt quite discombobulated when she looked down and noticed that she was still fully clothed and was lying on one of the huge sofas in the lounge. Someone must have covered her with blanket. What on earth was she doing here? She groaned as she realised that she may have had too much to drink last night and had passed out.

Liv placed a tray laden with china mugs, a milk jug and a large cafetière on the coffee table next to the sofa. The smell of strong coffee nearly made Debs heave.

'Morning, beautiful. Coffee?'

Debs certainly didn't feel very beautiful. Her hair was matted to her head in clumps and her mouth felt gritty. She looked totally confused to be on the sofa.

'You passed out, mate. We tried to wake you to get you up to bed, but you were having none of it. So we decided to leave you.'

'Bloody wine is strong over here,' Debs grumbled. She put her hands to her head and winced.

'Yes, and the tequila shots you drank afterwards may have had something to do with it too.'

'I don't even like tequila!'

'That's what you said in Corfu twenty-nine years ago. It didn't stop you getting drunk on it then, and it certainly didn't stand in your way last night!' Liv laughed.

'How come you look so fresh and glowing this morning?'

'I've been up for hours, hon. I stopped drinking after dinner and moved on to water. Been for a run around the marina and sat on the beach and watched the sun rise. I'm making the most of every minute I'm here.' She flung herself on the opposite sofa and alternated between sipping a glass of iced water with lemon and a mug of coffee.

Fiona tottered into the room in a black silk kimono and matching slippers and stretched her arms above her head. 'Oh, what a lovely night. The food was divine. How great it was to catch up properly after all these years. Oh my bed was sooo comfy. I've slept like a log. I think not having to keep one ear constantly listening out for Mum has done me the world of good.'

Debs burped loudly. 'Oh God! I'm so sorry, but I have awful indigestion. It must have been all the cheese.'

Fiona laughed. 'And the bread and the garlic prawns and the meat, *and* everything else you ate.'

'Oh God! I remember now! I was a right pig, wasn't I? I wish I could control myself when it comes to food. I just can't say no.'

'You just have to say NO, Debs.' Liv laughed.

'I honestly feel like I'm not in control. Since Dave went off with Perfect Fucking Penny, I really don't know what to do with myself. All I seem to do is eat and drink, and that makes me unhappy, so I eat and drink more. Morning, Samantha.'

They all smiled at Samantha as she floated into the room in a multi-coloured kaftan and reached over to the tray to pour herself a coffee. She flung herself on the sofa next to Debs, who winced at the sudden movement. Her head hurt like hell.

'Who fancies going into Vilamoura today? We could have a wander round, have a late brunch, then spend an hour on the beach.'

'I'm up for that. I went for a run around there this morning. It looks lovely. Although nowhere was open then. I spoke to a fisherman who was taking a boat out and he said that it didn't start to come alive until around eleven-ish when the bars and restaurants open up,' said Liv.

'Chatting men up already?' asked Samantha.

Liv laughed. 'To be honest, I'd be happy if I didn't see another man for a while. My three needy males have put me off for life. I do miss the dog though. I love my Hector. He's the least needy in the whole family! All he asks is to be loved, fed, walked and have a belly rub from time to time. A bit like me really! He'd have loved a run along the marina this morning.'

'I could murder a full English breakfast to soak up all that booze.' Debs stretched and stood up.

'Shall we head in around ten thirty, then? We can walk from here. It'll take about fifteen minutes to gently stroll in.'

'Perfect,' they all replied in unison, although Debs wished they were going in a taxi.

MIKEY HAD ALREADY told them on their trip from the airport that Vilamoura was purpose-built as a golfing centre in the 1980s. As the ladies walked to the town they passed a number of exclusive golf courses and large hotel complexes. When they reached the marina they could see it housed a variety of boats, from small fishing dinghies to million-dollar yachts with staff and jet skis on the back.

'Wow. Look at the size of that. Who could possibly own a yacht that looks like that?' Debs was seriously impressed.

Outside the Tivoli Marina Hotel, the most stunning sleek black yacht was moored. While the girls swooned over it, imagining another life where they frequented this type of boat every day, the rumble of a throaty engine got nearer. When they turned to see what the noise was, a Ferrari, painted to match the boat, both bearing the name on their sides, pulled to a stop right next to the yacht.

Out of the car, the most elegant couple they'd ever seen appeared. The man and woman were dark-haired and tanned, and dripping in designer clothing and accessories, which Debs thought probably cost more money than her house.

Debs' jaw nearly hit the ground. 'Wooooooow! Who are they?'

Liv tucked Debs' arm into hers. 'Someone way out of our league, darling. Come on, let's get some brunch.'

As the friends meandered around the marina looking for somewhere suitable for brunch, they joked around, taking selfies and laughing loudly. They spotted a bar that overlooked the moorings and decided that they'd stop there. They ordered café au laits while they chose what to eat. The marina was the perfect place to people watch.

'Oh, it's lovely, isn't it?' Fiona said, and then she sighed. 'How the other half live. Although I'm surprised your George hasn't got a yacht out here, Liv.'

Liv laughed. 'Oh God, don't give him more ideas of how to be a pretentious nob. He's doing pretty well on his own!'

'Is everything OK at home, Liv?' asked Fiona. 'You've said a few things that make me think that all is not rosy in the Pemberton house.'

'Oh, we're OK, I suppose. I'm sure every mum gets fed up of her family from time to time.' She looked around at her friends in turn. 'Don't they?'

There was a moment or two of hesitation from her friends. 'Of course they do.' Fiona patted her hand.

Liv snatched it away. 'No need to be patronising. At least I have a husband and don't hide away behind my mother.'

A loud collective gasp went around the table.

'Shit. I'm so sorry, Fiona, that was totally unnecessary. Please forgive me!'

Fiona smiled tightly.

'I'm going to the toilet,' Liv announced.

She slammed the ladies' room door behind her as she stepped towards the wash-basins and looked in the mirror. What on earth made her say that to her friend? She was totally and utterly mortified. Fiona had enough going on in her life, caring for her mum full-time, and now Liv had been vile to her. For no real reason.

Although if Liv dug deep enough, she knew the reason. And it was because Fiona had been so very close to the mark with what she had implied. She knew they'd be talking about her and that she'd have to go back out there and face them. And, at some point, probably admit to why she had been so eager for them all to get together on this holiday.

'Come on, Liv. You've got this! Put your big-girl pants on and get back out there before it gets to be a bigger thing than it really is,' she scolded herself in the mirror.

As she headed back to the table, her friends' voices went quiet. She stood next to Fiona.

'Please, please, please forgive me. This is not about you. This is about me. You may have gathered that I'm going through some stuff right now and it's been really getting to me. I will share it when I'm ready, but that's not right now. But if I could take back what I said, and not see that hurt in your face, then I would. Please can we start over?' Liv reached out to take Fiona's hand. Her chin quivered.

Fiona held her head up high. 'Do you know what, Liv? We're all going through some shit right now, but we haven't taken it out on our friends. That's not what *we* do. Of course I forgive you, you daft cow. But do it again, especially when I need food, and I will slap you. You really shouldn't mess with me when I'm hangry.' She grinned and Liv's shoulders slumped in relief and they all laughed nervously.

After a hug, Liv whispered in Fiona's ear, 'I really am so sorry.' Fiona squeezed her hand and nodded.

The situation was diffused even further when the waiter came over to take their order. They filled the time before their food came with admiring two very handsome men in linen shorts and shirts, and matching mirrored sunglasses, who walked towards one of the larger yachts moored right by their restaurant and climbed aboard. There was a sign on the back of the yacht giving prices for morning, full-day or evening charter. Liv raised her eyebrows as an idea popped into her head.

'Good morning, ladies! Beautiful day.'

'Morning,' they chorused back.

Liv, who had always had a photographic memory, clocked the website for the charter company and logged onto the marina WiFi to get more details. She'd give Mikey a call later and ask him to negotiate a good rate. After all, that's what she was paying him for.

Brunch was served and it was absolutely delicious – though pricey.

'Bloody good job it was a nice meal,' Fiona grumbled as they shared the bill. 'It's geared up for the rich here, that's for sure.' Of all of them, Fiona was the most frugal, in both her younger years and since she'd had to quit her job to look after her mum. Luckily she had a certain amount of savings to live on, along with the sale from her mum's house, and a small carer's allowance would start to come into force soon too, now that they'd started to get things moving with a diagnosis. But she still needed to watch her pennies.

'Come on, let's head off to the beach and have a lie in the sun for a bit, then we can head back to the villa for the afternoon.'

'Good idea, Liv, but can we get a taxi back? I don't think I could possibly walk anywhere after eating that full English.' Debs patted her stomach.

'I won't be able to eat anything till next week.'

On the way to the beach they walked past an ice-cream shop, and Debs was the first in the queue. 'Surely we can squeeze just a scoop in.'

'Debs, you're terrible.' Samantha laughed.

'I know. But you love me, right?'

They all giggled. It felt so good to be together and Liv hoped that the earlier episode could be forgotten. She was still feeling incredibly guilty about being so rude to her friend. What had she been thinking?

Chapter Thirteen

TWENTY-FIVE MISSED CALLS, ten voicemails and forty-seven text messages. And she'd only been gone for one and a half days. When Liv had turned on her phone to look at the yacht website, she noticed her call register and her heart sank. At that point, she'd thrown her phone in her handbag and tried to ignore it, but it had been eating away at her all the time she was lying on the beach – she couldn't switch off and relax at all. The first thing she did when she got back to the villa was to go to her room. She took a deep breath and got out her phone. She started to read the messages and felt sick to her stomach.

Mum, where is my Barcelona shirt?

Olivia, the dog has been sick…

Mum, James keeps being nasty to me.

Olivia, how am I supposed to work and look after the kids?

Mum, I don't like what Dad has ordered from the takeaway...

There wasn't one message asking how she was and whether she was having a nice time. She felt that she had become invisible to her family as a person, and was just their skivvy. And she'd had enough. She *had* to have a plan for when she got home. She couldn't go back to the same life she had left behind. She wouldn't be able to face it.

She couldn't bring herself to read one more text, so she deleted them all, wiped the call history without listening to any of the voicemail messages, switched her phone off and threw it in the top drawer of the chest in her bedroom. She knew that shutting the problem away wasn't going to solve anything, but she had to think about how she could change things to make life better.

She hoped that chatting with the girls would help her. She tied back her long platinum, high-lighted blonde hair with a sparkly clip, grabbed a sarong from the wardrobe and headed to the terrace. She needed some sun and some time to think.

WHEN FIONA GOT back to the villa, she also shot up to her room. She desperately wanted to speak to Brenda so called her on her mobile. It was lovely of Brenda to give out her personal number, knowing how anxious leaving her mum behind had made Fiona feel.

'Hello, Fiona, my lovely. How are you getting on?'

Brenda had such a wonderful way with people. Her soothing voice immediately made Fiona feel better; she could feel the stress melting away. Fiona thought Brenda should do her own meditation recordings.

'Oh, it's lovely, thank you. Lovely to spend time with the girls again. But how is Mum? I can't stop worrying about her, to be honest.'

'Fiona, you need to trust that she's safe and she's well. We're looking after her and she's enjoying her time here. When I finished work last night I went in and sat with her for an hour before going home. I sat and held her hand, and we talked about all sorts of things. We sat with the radio on and she was singing away.'

Fiona placed a hand on her heart. 'Oh, how fabulous. Mum loves to sing. It's amazing how she can remember the words to songs but can't remember other things.'

'Yes, it is. It's because a different part of the brain is used for singing. Like how a different part of the brain holds long-term memories to that which holds short-term memories. The brain is so complicated, but it's good to keep it active. Singing is really good for dementia patients. And they sometimes get up to have a dance too, like yesterday. It's so lovely to see them enjoying themselves.'

'That sounds wonderful. Thank you for being so kind to Mum. You don't have to spend your own time with her. I'm sure you have enough to do.'

'I do, but I know that you'd want to know that she's being well cared for, and it's important for you to feel that.'

'Thank you, Brenda. You really are one in a million. I don't know how to repay you for your kindness.'

'I'm sure we'll think of something.' Brenda laughed. 'I don't mean to be rude, but I really have to fly as I'm supposed to be doing a tea run right now and I'll be getting told off if I'm late. It's really good to talk to you, Fiona. Call any time. I mean that. In fact, why don't we do a FaceTime call with your mum one of the days. Then you can see for yourself just how she's getting on. Bye, lovely. Enjoy your holiday.'

Fiona felt so much better once she'd spoken to Brenda. She felt overwhelming gratitude towards this kind-hearted woman, who she'd only known for a short time, who was investing her precious time in someone else's mother.

SAMANTHA HEADED STRAIGHT to the kitchen when her phoned pinged. She saw that she'd got a text from Peter.

Mum, please transfer some money into my bank account. Funds running low.

Samantha read the text three times. This was the first time she'd heard from him in two weeks, even though she'd sent regular texts to him. And now, this. No, 'Hi, Mum, how are you?' No kiss at the end. And no 'please' and 'thank you'. This just wasn't right. She tutted loudly as Debs came into the kitchen and opened the fridge door.

'You OK, Sam? Fancy a snack?'

'I'm fine, thanks.' Her voice wobbled.

Debs turned to her, and the tear that rolled down Samantha's cheek made it clear she wasn't fine.

'Come on, honey, come and sit down. What's going on, Sam? You can tell me.'

Liv and Fiona entered the lounge at that point too.

'Sam, what's happened?' Liv frowned, sitting the other side of her, rubbing her arm.

'Oh I'm just being a silly old thing,' Samantha replied, wiping the tears from her cheeks and grabbing a tissue to blow her nose.

'Come on, a problem shared and all that. Perhaps we can help,' Liv suggested.

'It's just Peter. He doesn't speak or call for weeks on end, even though I text him all the time asking him how he is and what he's up to. I just got a text from him asking for money.' She held her phone up and showed them the message.

'When was the last time you actually spoke to him?' Liv asked.

'It was about two weeks ago and he said that he'd done a Tesco online shop and needed my bank details to pay for it.'

'Cheeky little bugger!' Debs chuntered under her breath, but it came out a lot louder than she intended.

'I asked him what he'd spent his allowance on. I give him four hundred pounds a month, and that's just pocket money. All his bills are paid separately. He said that he gets through that in no time going out drinking and eating with his mates. I suggested that he gets himself a part-time job, maybe in a bar or in a local shop or something, and he told me to get lost. He said that he shouldn't have to do that when his dad's life insurance is sitting in the bank. He doesn't realise that most of that went towards paying off the huge debts his father left behind, so that we could afford to continue to live in our family home.'

She took a deep breath. It was the first time she'd admitted to anyone what had really happened around the time that her husband died. That while struggling to cope with her own grief as well as that of her child, she had bailiffs knocking on the door and loan sharks who had scared the living daylights out of her demanding payment or threatening to repossess items from the house. She felt her chest tightening as those memories rose to the surface.

'Oh, Sam, you poor thing. Why didn't you tell us? Perhaps we could have helped.' Liv put her hand on Samantha's back.

'I was ashamed of Robert, Liv, and to be honest I was ashamed of myself for not seeing what was in front of my face. I thought he was out working hard for his family, when all the time he was just getting more and more into debt. It all started to make sense. He used to run to get the mail from the postman before I could see it, and at first I thought it was a game between us, but then I

Chapter Fourteen

'PERHAPS YOU NEED a bloke in your life, Sam. Maybe that's what you need.' Fiona thought she had the answer.

'Hmmm, really? You think so?' Liv murmured doubtfully. 'Actually, you can have mine. One careful lady owner from new.' They all laughed loudly.

'Oh God, the thought though! I really don't think I can be bothered. And what if I meet someone and really like him and he turns out to be a complete arse? I've heard so many horror stories of people who meet blokes online who turn out to be married or a total tosser. A friend of mine, Grace, had some horrific experiences when she tried internet dating. I really don't think I could put myself through all that. Although then she met her Vinnie when he knocked on her door one day to do some work at her house, and they're all loved up and married now. But then it *does* work for some people. There was a lady on the TV the other day who'd met her second husband online and they were very happy together. Oh, I don't know.'

'You need a dog not a man.' They all laughed again at Liv's statement. 'Honestly, I get more affection from Hector than the rest of my family put together. And he's way less needy. And if you get a dog, it gets you out of the house and back to nature.'

'That's a good point. I do need to get out more. One of the things I wanted to ask for your help with while I'm here is how I can start to make new friends. It's hard, and I know I have you guys, but I'm a good few miles from the nearest one of you and I need to make more friends locally. I know I do a bit of admin work from home from time to time, and that has its advantages, but with never going anywhere but the local Tesco, I don't get the chance to meet anyone.'

'Why don't we do some brainstorming when we get out of the water and come up with some new ways to meet people?' Liv suggested. 'Some of our ideas might be crap, but we might come up with a gem between us.'

'Now that sounds like a plan!' agreed Samantha. 'I'm going to get out, dry off and fetch a notepad and we can write some ideas down. Since

I've been going through this bloody menopause my head is like a sieve. If things aren't written down, I'll never remember them.'

Debs joined in the conversation. 'Oh, don't talk to me about the menopause. When I wake up in the morning my hair is wringing wet, and I'm showering twice a day. Honestly, between the hot flushes and the night sweats, and the paranoia and the anxiety, I feel like a different person these last few years. It's no wonder Dave left me. Things that never used to bother me really play on my mind now.'

'Perhaps actually the reason Dave left you is because he doesn't know a good thing when he has one and also because PFP waved her bloody tits and shook her arse in front of his face once too often,' Liv retorted hoping that she was able to reassure Debs that the split wasn't her fault.

'It's good to know that other people are going through the same thing though, isn't it, girls?' Samantha said.

'Speak for yourselves. I might be fifty and single,' said Fiona, 'but I've been on the pill for the last ten years, which means that I don't have periods and it delays the menopause so I'm sticking with that for the time being. The nurse has said that it's fine to do that for the moment, and I'm not complaining. Especially when I hear you lot moaning about your symptoms.'

'I don't blame you, hon.' Debs rolled her eyes.

The sound of water trickling made them all turn around with a start. There, on the far side of the garden, was a sight that they couldn't help but gawp at. A man, in a pair of cut-off denim shorts, his naked bronzed chest glistening with sweat, was watering the garden with a hosepipe he had grasped in his left hand. He ran his other hand through his hair and then stroked his short but perfectly groomed beard.

Debs gulped. '*Oh! My! God!* Who? Is? That? *He! Is! Gorgeous!* Shit! I hope he wasn't listening to our conversation about the menopause. Although I'm a whole different type of damp now!'

They roared with laughter and he turned towards the noise. As he neared the terrace to water the plants dotted around the edge, he introduced himself.

'Sorry to disturb your afternoon, ladies, but I am Eduardo. I believe you met my brother Josep last night. He cook for you. I am the gardener and water the garden and flowers.'

As he walked past Debs he winked at her and her stomach turned a somersault. She didn't think that she'd ever seen a man that beautiful in her life.

She muttered 'Phwoar!' and thought it was under her breath, but giggles from Liv made her cringe when she realised that she'd said it out loud.

'Ooh you're in there, Debs,' Liv said.

'In my dreams. Why would a man who looked like that ever look at someone like me?'

'Oh Debs, please do stop putting yourself down. You've always been the one out of all of us who had men flocking to you. You are so very pretty but you can't see it. What *do* you see when you look in the mirror? I'm pretty sure you're looking at something different to what we see.'

'Ha. I can't remember the last time I looked in a mirror.' She laughed it off.

'Seriously?' Liv asked.

'Yes. I hate what stares back at me, so I don't look. Why would I?'

'But, Debs, you always look so gorgeous. Your hair is beautiful – so glossy and thick – I'd kill for hair like that. You have an hourglass figure that I've always wished I had, rather than this stick-thin straight-up-and-down body. And you have the longest legs of any of us.'

'My legs are probably the only thing I do like, to be honest.' She laughed. 'But I'd swap everything else in a heartbeat.' She looked down at her hands and twiddled a tissue she'd been holding.

'Well, Eduardo was definitely liking what he saw. The rest of us didn't get a look-in. You should get in there.'

'Don't be ridiculous!'

'Seriously, babe, he couldn't take his eyes off you.'

'Well, it's a nice thought that someone like him could fancy a fat old bird like me. I'm going to have a snooze now and dream about him. What a good-looking family! Wonder if there's any more of them.'

'Ooh yes, there might be more,' said Liv. 'How fabulous but I'd rather a nice dog instead. However, an afternoon snooze in the sun sounds perfect. I'm absolutely shattered, even though we've done bugger all since we've been here but eat and drink. I think it's when you stop; life is so busy at home and simply relaxing feels exhausting. It clearly does you good. Enjoy your snooze. Hope you've all put your suntan lotion on. Laters.'

Liv pulled her sun hat over her face and put in her headphones. She was listening to a meditation app, which she was loving, because when she was at home, every time she put in her headphones someone tapped her on the shoulder to ask her something trivial, and would nearly give her a heart attack. She was enjoying just being herself on this holiday. Not someone's mum, not someone's wife, but just her. And the only person in her family she was missing right now was Hector.

'COOEE!' THEY ALL woke with a start around an hour later.

'Mikey, how are you?' Liv sat up and shielded her eyes from the glare of the bright sunlight to chat to him.

'I'm good, ladies, how the devil are you? Enjoying the sunshine, I see. How are you finding the villa?'

'We are loving it here. Couldn't have had a better place.' Fiona drawled and slowly raised her arm in a half-hearted wave. 'Soooo relaxing.'

'I'm so glad to hear that. I'm off to pick up my parents from the airport, so I thought I'd pop in on the way. They'll be staying next door and I've just been to the shops to get them some bits so they don't have to go to the supermarket for a day or two.'

'That's kind of you. How long are they out here for?' Liv enquired.

'Well, they're booked in for a week. But I wondered whether I could ask you a favour while they're here. If you see us around at all, could I ask you to call me Mike, or Michael?'

Liv sat up and frowned. 'Can I ask you why?'

'OK, so here's the thing. I think I told you that I live with Bernardo, who owns the villa property company.' Liv nodded. 'He's not just my boss, but my erm, well, partner too. My life partner. Mum and Dad don't know this and think that I'm straight. I've never managed to pluck up the courage to tell them. I honestly don't think they'd react well if they knew, so it's just easier to pretend that we're housemates. I know it probably sounds a bit mad to you, but that's how it has to be. Bernardo isn't very happy about it either, but I know he'll come round.'

'But what a shame you can't be honest with them. Are you sure they wouldn't handle it better than you think?' Liv asked. 'If it was one of my boys I wouldn't care less what his sexuality is as long as he's happy.'

'I really don't think they would. Dad's very old school and Mum goes along with everything he says. And they've been bugging me for years to give them grandchildren. I've never wanted to tell them that it's not going to happen.'

'Oh, Mikey, perhaps they'd surprise you though,' she said hopefully.

'I just can't. It's only for a few days so it would

be great if you could just do the Mike thing, rather than Mikey. Mikey sounds a bit, well, gay! Anyway, I knew I'd be able to trust you lovely ladies. I need to pop off to the airport now. We might not even see you while they're here but just in case – don't forget.'

'We won't, Mikey!' they chorused.

He gave a little wave as he got into his bright red convertible VW Golf, but he looked nervous.

'SHALL WE GO out for dinner this evening? Or do you want to stay here again? There's loads of food in the fridge we can put out, or we could head off and find a nice restaurant. Does anyone have a preference?' Debs asked.

'How about we eat here tonight? We've already been into Vilamoura today. Then we could find somewhere at the marina tomorrow night,' Liv suggested.

'Perfect for me,' Fiona said. 'I can stay in my cossie till later, then have a quick shower and put some comfies on. I'm getting old, I know, but I do like a nice pair of comfies.'

'Me too!' Samantha said. 'The good thing about living on your own is that no one gives a shit what you look like. I have more clothes to stay in than I do to go out in. There's nothing nicer than a new pair of pyjamas.'

They all laughed and agreed.

'I'm happy to throw a pesto pasta dish together and then perhaps we can have that with the cooked meats that are in the fridge. There was fresh bread delivered this morning and cheeses and stuff. We'll be able to make a meal out of that, won't we?' Liv asked.

The girls spent a leisurely afternoon hanging around the pool, snoozing, reading and chatting. They were all looking forward to another easy evening; when the villa was this gorgeous, they really wanted to make the most of it.

Debs went up to her room to grab her paper-back. The French doors leading to her balcony were still open from when she went out this morning and she wandered out onto the large roof terrace. She leant on the railings, admiring the sea view, when into her line of vision walked Eduardo. God, he really was drop-dead gorgeous with his grey hair and suntanned face. The phrase 'Silver Fox' popped into her mind. He looked up at her and his face lit up. His smile, as he flashed his bright white teeth, contrasting against his sun-tanned face, was dazzling. Her tummy fluttered as if there were a million butterflies trying to escape.

He walked to the bottom of her balcony and she felt as if she could almost reach out and touch him.

'Good afternoon again, Eduardo.'

'Good afternoon, miss. Are you having good holiday here in Portugal?'

'We, erm, yes. We're having a lovely time, thank you.'

He lingered, waiting for her to say something else, but her words seemed to dry up. He smiled, picked up the hosepipe again and saluted her before he carried on watering the hanging baskets.

She picked up her book and took it downstairs. In a split-second decision, instead of going through the lounge and onto the terrace, she walked through a side door and into the area of the garden where Eduardo had been. He was nowhere to be seen, so she turned and headed towards the terrace when a sudden cough from behind her startled her.

'Whoa!' She put her hand to her chest.

'I'm so sorry, I didn't mean to make you scared.'

'That's OK, it's fine. Honestly.'

She smiled. He really was incredibly handsome. As he smiled back, she noticed that he had the twinkliest eyes she had ever seen.

'I wanted to give you this.' He held out his hand, in which a beautiful crimson flower sat. It was a cross between a poppy and a hibiscus. 'Flor da Romãnzeira, or you might know it as a pomegranate flower. We have many fruit trees here in this garden, lemons, limes, but the pomegranate flower is the prettiest. A beautiful flower for a beautiful lady.' He held the flower up to her head, tucked it behind her ear, bowed and walked away. She stared dreamily at the space he had vacated and wondered whether love at first sight was really a thing.

She walked round to the terrace and Liv raised an eyebrow. She reached up and touched the flower.

'Pretty, Debs. It suits you. Did you pick it in the garden?'

'It's a Flor da Romãnzeira.'

'Oh, get you! How on earth do you know that's what it's called?'

'Eduardo gave it to me.'

'Ooh, I bet that's not all Eduardo wanted to give to you, judging by the way he was looking at you earlier,' said Samantha as she came over to the sunbed area.

'Don't be vulgar, Samantha. It doesn't become you,' said Debs, before she and her friends all laughed at her attempt to be prissy.

'How do we feel about going into the gypsy

market in Quarteira tomorrow?' Samantha asked. 'I've been doing some research. Don't roll your eyes at me, Olivia Pemberton.' She'd anticipated Liv's reaction before she'd even made it and more laughter ensued. 'The Internet says that there are loads of stalls selling traditional handmade goods and local produce. Apparently, it's one of the most popular markets in the Algarve.'

'It sounds great,' said Fiona. 'I love a market. I'd love to see if they have any leather handbags, I do love a holiday handbag.'

'Fantastic, that's tomorrow's excursion planned. How lovely! See, I might be boring for staking out the neighbourhood, but at least we're getting to do some nice stuff while we're here. Right then, I'm going up for a nap. I never knew doing nothing was so exhausting.'

They agreed to meet up at six p.m. for drinks. Cocktail hour seemed to be becoming a thing.

Chapter Fifteen

LIV HAD RUN herself a long luxurious bath and must have dozed off at one stage because she heard a deep rumbling noise and realised that it was coming from her. She couldn't remember the last time she'd felt as relaxed. It was so nice, to have a bath in peace and quiet, without anyone yelling up the stairs at her asking where their SuperDry top or their golf trousers were. All the males in her life, except for Hector, expected to put something in the wash and for it to be back and hanging up in the wardrobe within a couple of hours.

She had hoped that them having that bit of independence while she was away might make them think twice about their constant demands but from the messages she'd had already, it would appear that wasn't the case. She hoped they were missing her, not just for what she did for them but for who she was. She knew that Hector would miss her but also knew that Steve from ChasinTails loved him nearly as much as she did and would make sure he was fed and got his walk twice a day. It came to something that she would trust this job to someone outside of the family rather than one of them. Said it all, really.

It was her own fault, in a way. She thought back to when they were first married and how they'd both worked so hard to pay their bills and afford the house that George wanted them to buy to make them look good to their friends. She couldn't have cared less where they lived as long as they were happy and together. At that time she was working as a personal shopper in a department store. She loved that job, and was very good at it, earning a huge amount of commission and a number of awards from the company for being one of the highest-performing staff members.

When George's business had taken off she'd been a huge help behind the scenes, and was there at his beck and call. He concentrated on the business side of things and she arranged all the extravagant social events, which were so important in his world. They were the perfect partnership. He talked through all his business decisions with her and she felt part of a very special team. It had been so exciting when everything came to fruition and they could expand into other markets, which had opened up huge opportunities neither of them thought would ever be possible.

When Olivia discovered she was pregnant with James, George was insistent that he wanted her to take it easy and not work. It wasn't an easy decision for her to make, but she felt it was something she'd go back to when James was a few months old.

Olivia bit her lip as one of her most precious memories hit her hard, right in the stomach. She was sitting in the nursery in the middle of the night feeding James, when she felt another presence in the room. She looked up and saw George watching them from the doorway, totally mesmerised. He walked over to them, knelt at her feet, kissed James on his tiny button nose and her on her forehead, as if they were his most cherished possessions and that life couldn't get any better. The look of pride on his face at that particular moment had always stayed with her.

She'd not noticed when that feeling had left him. She supposed it must have gradually slipped away after the euphoria of parenthood had eased off, after disturbed sleep and leaking boobs. She felt that after a few months he went on to see them as a bit of an inconvenience in his life.

With one thing and another, the new house and

a new baby kept her busy and before she knew it three years had gone by. At that time she had been thinking about getting in touch with her previous employer, to see if there were any jobs available, when she found out she was pregnant with Seb. After that, there didn't seem to be any point.

George's involvement with his family lessened when Seb was young. He wasn't the easiest child, and his colic had meant that sleep was something that didn't happen for long in that house. It was hard. But at a time when they should have pulled together, sadly they seemed to pull a little further apart.

Taking on the role of the perfect mother and the perfect businessman's wife, Olivia spent her days making sure that the house was always tidy, the children were always clean, beautifully clothed, attended the best nurseries and then schools, got to all the right extra-curricular clubs, and that George didn't have to worry about a thing on the home front.

Thinking about it now, she wished she'd played things differently back then and insisted on returning to work when the children were young, and even in the gap in between them. She knew she could have money for anything she wanted; and anything she didn't want but George wanted her to have – but it wasn't about him giving her money. It was about being *worth* something. It was about being important enough in her family's lives for her opinions to be considered. Perhaps earning her own money would be a start. It might make her feel more valued. If she wanted to repair her fractured family, it was about time she stood up for herself.

Being away was clearing her head enough for her to start thinking about how she could make some changes. She couldn't think straight at home. Her head was always full of crap, of everyone else's *stuff*. Where the kids had to be at what time, what they needed to have with them, what homework they had to do and by when. Food was a constant demand from everyone. She'd had no idea that growing boys would eat non-stop, and she was expected to prepare a meal at the drop of a hat if George brought a colleague home for dinner. Laundry was a huge chore; their washing machine and tumble dryer were constantly on. When George went away on a business trip, he even expected her to pack for him.

And then there was the dog who she loved dearly, but who had been left to her despite the claims from the boys and George that they would share in everything if she allowed them to have a dog. The walks, the feeding, the shit shovelling, the wiping of muddy paws and the repetitiveness of every day was really getting her down.

She felt that in her family's eyes she was only there to look after them. They never saw her as a person in her own right. She had been a complete fool over the last few years and it was time she made a stand. She was determined she wouldn't go back to that life. Time away hadn't made her heart grow fonder, it had hardened her heart and, although she loved her family desperately, there were going to be some huge changes on the horizon that they weren't going to like at all.

After carefully blow drying and then straightening her hair, and applying a slick of mascara to her false lashes, Olivia swept some blusher across her cheekbones to enhance the sun-kissed glow she already had from lying by the pool that day. She took a deep breath at the top of the stairs, and held her shoulders back. She could do this. And these wonderful ladies she was surrounded by right now might just be able to help her get back on the right track.

LIV GLANCED ACROSS the room at Debs standing at the window, looking out, with a glass of red wine in her hands, and wished she could be more like Debs. Debs always seemed so confident in her own skin and, yes, she carried a little extra weight, but still looked stunningly gorgeous.

George was always quick to point out to Olivia when she'd put on a couple of extra pounds and suggest she spend a bit more time at the health and fitness club they were members of. Cheeky git, when he had that paunch lots of middle-aged men had that hung over the top of his trousers in a most unattractive manner; the belly that came from a few years of too much good food and drink. When she'd dared to suggest that he could maybe spend a bit more time in the actual gym rather than the clubhouse, he told her that he didn't have all the time in the world to swan about all day like she did, and that his time in the clubhouse was business and therefore a necessity. Yeah, of course it was! He must think she was a fool to believe him.

Debs was staring out the window and hadn't noticed Liv watching her. As always, Debs looked alluring and sexy. She had an air about her that Liv had never possessed in all her years. It was strange how some people had *it*, and some didn't, and Debs had it in abundance. Debs had clearly been unhappy since she and Dave had split up, and she had seemed to have lost a little of her sparkle. Liv hoped that these few days away would help her friend get back her fizz.

It was strange how women were never happy with themselves, Liv mused. The way they were all envious of what others had, whether they were friends or not. Liv had always thought Debs was the prettiest of the group and she still was. Liv was striking, yes, she knew she was, but none of it was natural these days. There was nothing that couldn't be enhanced or lifted or tucked at a price.

'Hey, Debs, you're looking very serious there!'

'Ah, Liv. I was thinking what Dave would have thought of this villa. I know I shouldn't be thinking about him, but after being together so long, it's like my brain will never stop wondering about him and what he'd be thinking or doing if we were still together.'

She looked so sad. Liv walked towards her and rubbed her arm to comfort her.

'I suppose it's a habit that you have to try to break. It must be so hard after all those years. I can't imagine how you must feel after what happened.'

'I know he went off with PFP behind my back, and I should hate him, but I don't, you know, Liv. You can't suddenly hate someone you loved so much, just like that, can you? I just feel so bloody sad most of the time that our lives have come to this. I even wonder what I'd do if he told me he'd made a huge mistake and wanted to come back. I think I'd say yes, you know, and I'd try really hard this time to keep him happy. I could try harder to lose some weight. I know that's something he's not been happy with me for. And I'd make more of an effort with myself. Go out more often. Go on dates together. I'm sure we could get things back on track if PFP would just take her skinny little arse and fuck off out of the picture.'

Liv smiled. Debs always did have a way with words.

'Well, I know there's a very fine line between love and hate, Debs, but maybe it's time to look forward now and not backwards. If you want to lose some weight, do it for you and not for anyone else. And if it does happen, then that's great, but if it doesn't, perhaps you need a plan B. Perhaps we just need to find you a new man. Someone to put a smile back on your gorgeous face.'

'I know you're right, Liv, but it's just bloody hard. I literally have no one now and could you imagine going out dating again? Seriously? We never had kids because we were always enough for each other, but now I really regret it! I just want someone to need me.'

She picked up the bottle of red wine and refreshed her glass. 'Don't worry, I'll snap out of it. I was just having a moment.'

'And you are absolutely entitled to have a moment any time you like, and we're all here to help you through this, Debs. It's ridiculous though, isn't it? I feel like my family need me way too much and can't do anything for themselves. I wonder if we're ever truly happy or if we're constantly looking for something that doesn't exist. Perhaps we all need to actually work out the things that really do make us happy and strive for them. Otherwise, if we never know what makes us happy, how are we ever going to reach that point? We'll be constantly looking for something we won't be able to recognise!'

'Christ, that was profound. I think I need another drink after that little outburst!'

They laughed and Liv was pleased to see Debs smile again. She had looked so sad a few moments ago.

'Anyway, is that footsteps I hear? The others must be joining us.'

Chapter Sixteen

SAMANTHA REALISED SHE must have looked a bit gloomy when she came down.

'What's up, hon?' Liv asked her. 'Something happened?'

'Nothing in particular. Oh, lots of things at the same time. I tried to sleep but my brain wouldn't shut off.' She took a deep breath. 'I didn't know whether to say anything to you, but I'm driving myself bonkers. I'm so fed up with my life, girls. I rarely go out at home, and being here with you guys has made me realise how much I love having company and even getting ready to stay in, let alone go out. I live in my pyjamas or a pair of tatty old trackie bottoms at home because what's the point of dressing up to stop in if no one is going to see me? Since Peter went to uni, I don't think I've had a night out. Not even once that I can remember. I've realised that I put my life on hold for a long time for my family and now they've gone I have nothing. I spend my evenings surfing the internet, shopping on Amazon and spending money on things I really don't need. It makes me happy for the split second when I buy it and then two minutes later I regret it.'

'Get your notepad, Samantha. Let's do some mind mapping and write down some ideas for you to get out and about. You *should* get yourself a dog, you know.' Liv smiled. 'I think Hector is my soul mate. I miss him more than my family, if truth be known.' She looked round at her friends and they all looked really serious. 'Only joking!' She laughed, nervously fiddling with her necklace. 'Or if you're not sure about getting a dog of your own, perhaps you could put yourself up as a foster home. Loads of dogs need temporary homes, while they're looking for the right one.'

'I honestly don't think I could do that, Liv. I'd get too attached to them and then wouldn't want to give them away. It would be heart-breaking.' She shook her head. 'I do like the idea of having a dog though. A little pal of my own to chatter away to and to snuggle up with on the sofa of an evening.'

'So, come on then. Shout up with ideas, everyone.' Liv was bossy when she wanted to be. 'Nothing too daft, let's get all the ideas out and then we can go through each in more detail and see what suits. And I'm putting "get a dog" at the top.'

'I think now *is* the right time for me to get a dog. I have plenty of time on my hands and I'm at home most of the day so they wouldn't get left on their own much. So, number one – get a dog!' Samantha started to scribble.

'Number two – Salsa dancing. Get it on the list. I've always fancied that. I'll get pre-dinner drinks sorted,' said Fiona, sashaying her way towards the kitchen and clicking away at imaginary maracas. 'Everyone OK with G&T?'

There were approving nods all round.

'Wouldn't I feel an idiot going on my own though?' Samantha asked.

'The idea is that you go alone, so that you meet people. You need some new friends in your life. It might take a bit of courage at first, but surely there'll be other people in the same boat,' Debs added. 'I wish we lived nearer each other. I'd come with you. I could do with this list myself.'

Samantha added 'salsa lessons' to the list. 'We'll make a list for you too, Debs, before we go home,' she said.

'Ooh, ooh! Find a book club. You love reading. Watch that film on the TV with all the old stars who had a book club for over eighteen years and met up whatever happened. They had a whale of a time,' Liv suggested.

'I did look online but couldn't find one.'

'Well, start one then. Find a local café that might be interested in hosting one and then they can advertise it too.'

Samantha scribbled furiously in her notepad. 'I love that idea. I never even thought about starting one. What a nana I am.'

'A friend of mine did that four years ago. They're still together now and have become a really close group of friends. They have book club at a local café once a month, then meet up halfway through the month for a curry night, and they have days out shopping and even weekends away. It's hard at any time of your life to make friends, I think, so a group of like-minded people is great for friendship.'

Liv became animated as another idea popped into her head. 'Going back to the dog idea, you could get a rescue dog rather than a puppy, because let me tell you, I love my Hector, but puppies are bloody hard work. Nearly as much hard work as having a newborn baby. Oh, and you could join a local dog club. One of the single mums at school was talking about this recently and said that even though it's supposed to be all about the dogs socialising with each other, it's more about the dog owners, who have tons in common. They even go for group walks every fortnight too and sometimes have nights out without the dogs. That would definitely get you meeting new people *and* getting you out and about.' Liv smiled. 'Hector honestly is my best friend.'

'I really like that idea, Liv. I could start looking online to see if there are any rescue shelters locally. They might even like me to help out. I bet they're always looking for volunteers.'

'Put it on the list. Go dogging.'

Fiona laughed as she came back with four huge balloon glasses nearly overflowing. 'Did I hear someone mention dogging? I hear it's quite popular over Cannock Chase. I picked the lemon off the tree myself, by the way.' The aroma of fresh lemon was divine. 'Oh, Sam, look at your face.'

'What's wrong with my face, you cheeky cow?' Samantha bristled and squared her shoulders.

Fiona laughed. 'Nothing bad, darling. Your face is all lit up with happiness. When you came down you were full of doom and gloom and now your eyes are all sparkling with possibility and opportunity.'

'Oh, that's OK then!' Samantha laughed.

Fiona gave her shoulder a squeeze as she

walked past. 'It's lovely to see, Sam. I was a bit worried about you. I know how easy it is to get stuck in a rut. The more you don't go out and about, the less you want to do it.'

'Oh girls, what would I do without you?' Samantha said. 'I really have missed you all, you know. This trip is making me realise just how much.'

'Well, you might not say that when we've got further down the list. We've only just started.' Debs laughed and for some reason a snort came out, which made everyone fall about in a fit of the giggles. 'Laughing is so good for the soul. Coming away with you guys has made me realise that I haven't had a good laugh for a long time. You're like a breath of fresh air in my life. Since Dave went, I haven't laughed properly.'

'If you ask me, Debs, you didn't laugh that much *with* Dave in your later years of being married. You always used to moan about him when we spoke on the phone. Perhaps you're remembering something that wasn't really true. I remember it happening to me when I took Mum back to look at a house we used to live in. In my mind, it was a wonderful place which held some fabulous memories, and it was a big house which was really pretty, but when we went past it, it wasn't how I remembered it at all, and it looked tatty and unloved,' Fiona said. 'Perhaps it's time to stop blaming Dave for the things that aren't right in your life and start making your own luck and your own future.'

'Well, thanks for your wisdom, Oprah.' Debs laughed good-naturedly, but Sam saw a look on Debs' face that suggested what Fiona had said had hurt, even if, as Sam suspected, Debs knew it was the truth.

'What about holidays?' Fiona said to Sam, refocusing her attention. 'You could look at going on a singles holiday. You were only saying when we were talking about coming away here that you'd love to take more holidays but didn't really have anyone to go with. This might be a great opportunity for you.'

'Can't do that if I'm having a dog, though, unless I can find someone to look after them. Although I suppose there're kennels and pet sitters around.'

'Oh, that's easily sorted. Brenda was telling me that there is a singer that goes into the care home where Mum is at the moment, who also runs a doggy daycare and kennel place with her friend. I know it would be a decent drive from yours, but I know any dog would be well looked after. And there are all sorts of people around who might look after a dog, if it was a well-behaved one. At least that way you could still go on holidays.'

'It's definitely something to look into. There are so many places in the world that I'd still love to go to that. Perhaps I just need to have some company, without actually going on holiday *with* someone, if that makes sense.'

'I've just had another great idea.' Liv's eyes sparkled. 'Why don't you start a blog? There must be loads of people who feel the same way as you and you could try all these things out and then blog about it. Share your experiences to help and inspire others. Sometimes you can even get people to sponsor a blog and make some money from it too. I had a friend who was a travel blogger once and she got loads of press trips because the public want word-of-mouth endorsements these days rather than advertisements. She even got to go on some cruise holidays. And there are magazines who would pay you to write features about the places you visit. You always used to love writing and you were also really good at it. Why don't you mix your love of writing with travel *and* blogging? You'd be brilliant at it. You could get some holidays in the UK that were dog friendly and maybe some which were abroad, and have the best of both worlds.' Liv was on a roll. She loved helping others with ideas.

'OMG, that's a fab idea.' Fiona jumped up. 'I could help you set up a blog. I used to look after the website for the school before I packed it all in to look after Mum. We could even do it while we're here. Did anyone bring a laptop?'

'Yep, I brought mine,' Samantha said. 'I didn't want to tell any of you in case you thought I was mad, but I've got lots of things I'm bidding on, on eBay.' She felt ashamed that she was buying stuff she didn't need again. It had started to become a bit of an obsession, if truth be told, which she needed to clamp down on before it got out of hand. But she wasn't ready to admit that to anyone just yet. Perhaps if she had some other things to focus on, then this fascination with buying mindless crap to give her a temporary high might stop.

'This is so exciting.' Samantha's eyes twinkled and she grinned widely, imagining how this could take off. 'But am I not too old for this?'

'God, no! There must be so many people in the same boat as you who would love to read how you conquered your fear of doing things on your own and how you've made new friends and changed your life. You are *never* too old to change things in your life for the better. I just love the thought of this.' Liv was excited for her.

Samantha loved the idea of starting a blog. Wouldn't it be fabulous if someone else changed their life, because she inspired them? For what seemed like the first time in ages, Samantha was starting to get a fluttery feeling in her tummy. The stirrings of excitement. The promise of a future. Instead of her life being over, perhaps it was just the start of a whole new chapter.

'SO WHAT ABOUT you now then, Liv?'

Liv looked at the three faces staring at her, but particularly at Debs who had directed the question at her.

'What about me?' She stuck out her chin.

'You keep making quips about how Hector is the only one who isn't demanding of you. Are you happy with your lot in life?'

'Oh, my story will wait until another night. I'm fine, ladies. Nothing that a few days away with you gorgeous lot won't sort out. How about you, Fiona? How are things in your life?'

Fiona frowned. 'I don't want to talk about my life right now. I've come away to forget all about how crappy my life is.'

'Why, Fiona? Why is it so bad? You can tell us. Perhaps if you share, it might make you feel better,' said Liv.

'Well, don't say I didn't warn you. I'll give it a go, but don't think I haven't noticed you changing the subject, Liv. We will get back to you. Without a doubt.' She pointed two fingers towards Debs' eyes, then back at her own eyes and back to Debs again, and they all laughed. It would only stop Liv fending off the questions for the time being, though. 'We've finally had Mum's diagnosis and she's going rapidly downhill. Sometimes she remembers who I am, sometimes she doesn't. I'm her only daughter. It breaks my heart. My Mum is my favourite person in the whole world, she was the best mother to me that I could have wished for. Everything I took for granted on a daily basis in the past, and everything I've ever known, has been smashed to smithereens.' Her voice wobbled.

'Oh, darling. Can you get any help?' Samantha rubbed Fiona's shoulder.

'We are getting there but it's a very slow process. She's been going to a local dementia centre and spending the odd day there. But she hates me leaving her there and says they're all nasty to her. Yet when I ask the people how she's been, they tell me that she's had a ball and has been laughing and enjoying getting involved in their craft afternoons, and that she really enjoys the singer who comes in, and sings along to everything.'

'I saw a fabulous programme on the TV recently with that lovely girl Vicky McClure,' said Samantha. 'All about how singing in a choir is therapeutic for dementia patients. Perhaps there's a group nearby you could take her to. It also amazed me how it's not always old people who get dementia, which is something I'd always thought. There was a really young lad on it. It was heartbreaking. But Vicky was amazing. She'd got involved because of her Nanna and she wanted to raise awareness and help others. You should see if it's on catch-up on the TV. It really was a fabulous programme. Taught me an awful lot. It might give you some ideas for your mum too.'

'I'll definitely look into that, Samantha, thank you. It's a fab idea. She's staying at a home this week while I'm away. An absolutely lovely lady called Brenda is the manager. I met her at a support group I've been taking Mum to lately. Again, singing and dancing is at the heart of it all. She is just so lovely.' Fiona smiled as she thought about how kind and sympathetic to both herself and her mum Brenda had been. 'She's really made a special effort to make sure Mum is looked after this week. She thinks that I should put Mum in there more often, for some respite, but I feel so guilty doing that.'

She pressed her hand to her chest. 'Brenda also thinks that I should consider the fact that, at some stage, it might be better for Mum to live there permanently, but I don't think either of us are ready for that quite yet.' A tear trickled down Fiona's cheek. 'Sometimes I get so frustrated with her and then I feel really guilty too. She can't help any of it. It all makes me so very sad.'

'It must be so hard for you, but perhaps she's right, Fiona. It's an awful lot for you to manage on your own. And these are professionals who are trained to look after folks with this condition. Sometimes as a family member you are just too close, and outsiders who don't have the emotional ties that you have would do things differently and do what's best for the relative. I'm not saying that you don't do what's best for your Mum, darling, but these people know the right way to handle things and they don't get emotional because they're not attached in the same way that you are.'

Samantha's voice was soothing and she was talking a lot of sense. It made Fiona feel that perhaps there was another view and that maybe she should take a step back from the emotion of it all. She didn't want her mum to go into a home permanently right now, but she did know that her life was exhausting as a full-time carer and it would only get worse as time went on and this awful illness took even more of a hold.

She'd started hiding the house keys recently, as goodness only knows what would happen if her mum could get out when she wasn't being watched. Only last week Fiona had gone to the toilet and when she came back couldn't find her mum anywhere. She scoured the house and eventually went out the front to find her mum sitting in the car, looking at the set of car keys in her hand and saying that she couldn't remember what to do with them. Thank goodness Fiona had found her when she did, or it could have been a million times worse. Her blood pressure was sky high and her doctor had told her she needed to get it under control or she'd be too ill to look after her mum at all.

'I know you're right, Samantha. I just have to get my head round it. Brenda tells me that I need to get back to being Mum's daughter, rather than her carer, and make some special memories for us both – more for me, really, as Mum won't even remember most of them. She said we should have days out where we do lovely things together. She says I should work with dementia and embrace it, not try to fight it, and that I must also have a life of my own.'

'Brenda sounds like a very sensible person,' said Liv.

'She's a real gem.'

Liv knew they'd need to be chatting further to Fiona over the next day or so, but felt that she had unburdened herself enough for this evening. It was time to lift everyone's spirits a little.

'Is it time for another gin yet, ladies?' she asked.

'What a ridiculous question. It's always time for another gin.'

They laughed and held up empty glasses and encouraged Fiona to mix another round as she'd done such a sterling job with the first one.

FIONA STUMBLED INTO the kitchen laughing and Debs followed her through. She decided she'd better put some crisps, nuts and olives on the table before they were all too sloshed to enjoy the evening. Debs made a mental note to quiz Liv again later. She was too good at avoiding questions and diverting them to focus on others instead. Debs had a feeling that all was not OK in the Pemberton household. She would get to the bottom of it before this holiday was over if it killed her.

She shoved a handful of crisps into her mouth when she thought no one was watching, before taking the tray of snacks through to the lounge area. She didn't realise that Fiona was right behind her, so when Fiona spoke to her, she sprayed crisps everywhere and started to cough, going bright red in the face when one got stuck going down the wrong way! Liv jumped up and gave her a good thump on the back when she saw that she was struggling to breathe and grabbed a G&T from Fiona's tray, which Debs swiftly necked in one go.

'Christ, Debs. Steady on, girl! It might look like water but it isn't.' Liv gave Debs a good hard pat on the back.

'Don't worry about me, Liv. I can handle my booze! That I do know.'

As Debs had practically passed out again that afternoon around the pool, Liv doubted that very much! She was quite worried about the amount of alcohol Debs drank. Liv wasn't a huge drinker. She didn't need a drink to enjoy herself and because of that was pretty much always the one who drove so that George could have a drink. In fact, these days he didn't even offer, he just assumed that she'd drive. How times had changed.

Chapter Seventeen

'SO, ARE WE all ready?'

Liv glanced at Debs, who felt, and knew she probably looked, a little worse for wear. She didn't really want to go to the market, so she asked if they'd mind if she stayed behind.

'Of course we don't, hon. This is your holiday too. I hope you're feeling better later.'

The other three got into the taxi and waved goodbye.

Grabbing an orange juice from the fridge, she pulled a sunbed round to face the sun. That was vitamins C and D sorted for today. She hadn't slept particularly well, tossing and turning, alternating between heartburn and night sweats, so she just wanted to chill out, read and sleep, not be traipsing around a market in the heat.

After an hour of lying in the red-hot sun on the terrace, she decided that she needed to cool down. She'd been dying to get in that gorgeous pool since they'd arrived, but hadn't wanted to do that in front of the others. This might be the only opportunity she got.

She stripped off her sundress down to her costume, and sat on the side of the pool to get used to the cool temperature of the water before lowering herself into it. She gave a little gasp at how cold it was before lowering her shoulders underneath but once she was in, it actually felt really refreshing. Invigorated by the water, she was annoyed with herself for not doing this when the others had. Her insecurities about her weight had stopped her doing something she really enjoyed, and she realised now how daft it was. She was determined that she wasn't going to let that happen again. Perhaps it really was time that she took this situation in hand.

Resting her head on her hands, she looked around her, drinking in the surroundings. From this angle, in one direction, she could see the villa in its full splendour. The vibrant bougainvillea looked stunning against the white-washed villa walls and on each corner stood oleander trees in pots. She wished she had a pretty garden like this. Her garden was more of a back yard, all paved because Dave couldn't be bothered to mow a lawn. She'd tried her hardest to pretty it up over the years with potted plants dotted around and bedding plants adding a splash of colour in the summer, but she really missed a lush green lawn. Thinking about it now, she wasn't quite sure whether she'd actually told Dave that, or whether she'd just gone along with his plans for the easy route.

As she turned the other way, she couldn't believe that even though she'd seen it a few times now, the view beyond took her breath away. The sun sparkled on the turquoise blue sea, which was so still, and there wasn't a cloud to be seen in the deep blue sky. She could stare at it for hours. The sea made her feel happy. She didn't know why and giggled when she thought that perhaps she'd been a mermaid in a previous life.

She swam a few lengths and when she felt that she'd had enough, she decided to swim another ten. You couldn't keep doing the same things and expect a different result, and she had to start somewhere. As she walked up the pool steps, she shivered as she felt the presence of someone watching her.

'Eduardo!' she gasped.

'I'm sorry, I didn't mean to scare you. I should be watering. I am sorry.' He looked her up and down and smiled. 'You are very beautiful lady. Is Debs short for something?'

'It's short for Deborah.'

He took a step towards her. 'Then I will call you Deb-orah. Beautiful Deb-orah.'

Debs thought she was dreaming. How could a man who looked like this think that she, Debs from North Staffordshire – Debs who worked in a children's nursery and wore trousers and a polo shirt to work – be beautiful? She lowered her eyes to the floor.

He took another step towards her. He was so close now that she could smell his musky after-shave mixed with undertones of lemon and, if she wasn't mistaken, bergamot. He put his finger under her chin and raised her face so their eyes met.

'You are *very* sexy lady Deb-orah.'

A bead of sweat trickled between her breasts. The finger that was resting under her chin traced a line slowly and suggestively down her neck and stopped just above her cleavage. Debs realised she had been holding her breath. She felt a stirring between her legs that she hadn't felt for a very long time. What on earth was she doing?

'Your necklace is very beautiful,' he said, his hand coming to rest on the feather necklace she never took off.

Taking a step backwards, she steadied herself.

'Would you like some water, Eduardo?' she asked, not really knowing what to say to him. She wanted an excuse to get back to the sunbed so she could cover herself with her sarong. The last thing she wanted was him seeing her flabby tummy any more than he had to.

'Mmmm, please.'

God, how did he even manage to do that and sound so sexy? she wondered.

She grabbed the sarong from the back of the sunbed and tied it loosely around her chest, letting it drape over her costume. She filled a tall glass from the water jug on the table and passed it to Eduardo. He sipped at it, never taking his eyes off her.

'Do you live locally?' she asked, trying hard to fill the silence.

'Not far. I have an apartment in a place called Quarteira. How about you? Where do you live?'

She sat on one of the chairs and offered one to him. He sat next to her, his knee touching hers. God, she was glad she'd had her legs waxed before coming away. She hoped her bikini line wasn't sprouting hair as quickly as her legs usually did. She adjusted the sarong making sure it was covering up her lady bits.

'I live in a place called Burton-on-Trent in Staffordshire. Have you ever been to England?'

Still, he stared at her intensely. He made her feel very nervous.

'I have been to Birmingham. To the botanical gardens when I was at college. A nice place.'

'I've been to Birmingham many times, but I've not been there.'

'Very nice place. What is Burton-on-Trent like? Is it very pretty?'

Debs laughed to herself. She didn't think the words 'Burton-on-Trent' had ever been spoken so sexily. She didn't think he'd understand if she said that her home town had a permanent smell of Marmite in the air. She giggled nervously as she wondered how the word 'Marmite' would sound from his sexy mouth. God, she was hot. She didn't know if she was having a hot flush, if it was the weather affecting her, or this gorgeous man sitting beside her. She grabbed her portable fan off the table and tried to cool herself down.

'It's OK, I suppose. There're good and bad parts everywhere. We certainly don't have the weather that you have here in Portugal.'

'In Portugal we have good weather for most of the year. Even in December it can be eighteen degrees, and we still wear the shorts and the T-shirts.'

For a moment, they just smiled at each other, neither of them really knowing what to say next.

'Your brother is an excellent cook.'

'Ah, that he is. He has his own restaurant and catering business. He is very, as you say, success.'

'Successful,' Debs corrected.

'Thank you. My English is just OK.'

'Your English is brilliant. Way better than my Portuguese.'

'Then you should let me teach you.'

'I'd like that, Eduardo, thank you.'

'I will teach you some very easy ones right now. *Bom dia* is good morning, *boa tarde* is good afternoon, and *boa noite* is goodnight. Hello is *olá*, *tchau* is bye and *adeus* is goodbye. *Por favor* is please and *de nada* is you're welcome.'

'Gosh, could you write those down for me?' She picked up a notebook and pen from the table. 'I will learn them and teach the others.'

'Of course.' As he took the notebook and pen, his hand brushed against hers and a shiver ran from her toes to the tip of her head. 'If you wanted me to, I could teach you more.' He held her gaze and she felt like the world had stopped.

Debs couldn't speak. She wasn't sure whether she was imagining that he was being so flirtatious or if it was genuine. What seemed liked minutes, but was just seconds, passed by before he continued.

'Maybe I could pop by later, when I have finished my work when I break for the lunch.' He gazed at her seductively and she looked deep into his eyes, trying to work out if they were midnight blue or jet black. They were gorgeous, whatever the colour, with lashes that most women would die for.

Debs blushed *again*. She wasn't sure if it was Eduardo or the menopause, but she knew she was on fire right now and needed to get back in that pool to cool off and calm down very soon. What should she say to this? She wasn't sure how old he was, but from his looks alone, she felt that he was probably younger than her, yet he seemed really interested. She was flattered and the way he was looking at her alone was making her feel a million dollars. In a split-second decision she threw caution to the wind. What the hell? When in Portugal and all that.

'Thank you, Eduardo. I would like that very much. And please, call me Debs.'

'I would love that too, Deb-orah. Debs. Shall I see you at around one p.m. Does that suit you?'

'Yes, that would be great.'

He grinned and his whole face lit up and his

eyes twinkled mischievously.

'I must go and work, Debs. You are very – how you say – distracting to me.'

Debs couldn't believe this was happening to her. Eduardo was gorgeous and she was, well, just Debs.

'Até logo, Debs.'

He leant forward and kissed her cheek tenderly. She touched the place he had kissed and stared at him as he walked away, wondering how long it was until one p.m. and what time the girls would be back. She felt like a teenager looking forward to a date. What an amazing feeling. It was as if a million butterflies were dancing around in her stomach.

The trouble with being married for years is that you lose that feeling of lust and excitement. She and Dave had ended up more like brother and sister. They did still have a sex life, when they could be bothered, and when they made the effort it was perfectly nice, but it felt more like a chore to tick off the weekly to-do list. In hindsight, it's no wonder he fell for PFP. Maybe Debs made him feel like Eduardo was making Debs feel right now. But she wasn't going to think about them. She needed to get back in that pool and cool off. She made sure Eduardo wasn't around any more and ran and jumped in the water like a child. She was having fun and life was about having fun. She felt more carefree than she had for a long while.

ONCE SHE'D DRIED off, Debs texted Liv to see how they were getting on. She replied soon after:

Fab morning, we do miss you though. Hope you don't mind but we're going to have a late lunch and come back around four-ish. Is that OK with you? We don't want you to be on your own for too long, but don't want to rush back either. Let me know if that's OK. Wish you were with us x

At least Debs didn't have to be worrying about what time they would be back; she and Eduardo would have some time to get to know each other. As she thought this, that little flutter in her tummy happened again and she smiled to herself. She texted Liv back:

I'm fine. Enjoying some chilling time and pretending that this is my house and my normal life. Enjoy your lunch and don't rush back for me. I'm absolutely fine. See you later x

She picked up her paperback and read for a bit, but she couldn't really concentrate. She lay on her sunbed gazing out to sea, and let her thoughts run away with her. Just imagine if she did live in a place like this, where the sun shone most of the time and the pace of life was so calm.

In fairness, she knew she had it easier than most. She didn't have kids or a husband (any more) to run around after. She could please herself with what she ate and when she ate, although that wasn't really helping her. She looked down at her body and wished that her tummy wasn't so large. She really wanted to be able to do something about her weight, but, up until now, she didn't seem to have been in the right frame of mind. Maybe now the time was right for her. Maybe she should join a gym or at least go to a class. Though she was never a fan of gyms, if truth be told. The ones she'd been to in the past were full of skinny minnies, all looking at themselves in the mirrors with their perfect hair and make-up. She didn't feel she would fit in at a place like that.

Samantha had recently mentioned a slimming group called Busy Bodies in Little Ollington, which wasn't too far away from her house, run by her friend Grace, which was getting some great reviews. A couple of the girls from Samantha's work had been along and they were raving about it. It was all about healthy eating and gentle exercise. Apparently, they all met up and went on walks together too and it was supposed to be a great way to make friends. She made up her mind, there and then, that when she got back she was definitely going to go along.

It was time she started to think about herself and feel better about herself too. The other day she'd seen someone she thought she knew from about twenty-five years ago in a café, and she'd been dying to say hello, but she hadn't had the confidence to go over because she'd changed so much since they'd last seen each other. She hadn't wanted this person to look down their nose at her and think that she hadn't aged well at all. It was so silly. They used to be good friends, but she couldn't bring herself to do it.

If nothing else, this flirtation with Eduardo was making her realise that it was definitely time to deal with this issue of hers and take more care of herself. She went up to her bedroom and showered, washed and straightened her hair, slicked on a little mascara, and brushed some bronzer over her cheeks before heading back out to the terrace.

Eduardo appeared from the side of the villa. 'Olá, Deb-orah! How has your morning been?'

'Eduardo, hello.'

She felt ridiculously nervous. She knew she

shouldn't compare, but couldn't remember ever fancying Dave this much, even in the early days, and being so jumpy around him. They had drifted together after they'd met at college, and ended up getting married. She had loved him deeply, but there was none of this fluttery feeling with him.

'Can I get you a drink? Coffee, tea, or a cold drink – a beer or a wine?' She felt she needed some alcohol to still her nerves but also knew that was an area she needed to address. She drank way too much and was totally embarrassed that she'd passed out the other night. Up until now, she'd done that in private.

'A coffee would be perfect, thank you. I'm not a big drinker, and definitely not on my lunch break.'

Debs decided she would have coffee too. Drinking less booze would be helpful for her healthy life plan. And here, in Portugal, would be a great place to start with all the fabulous fruit and veg they had access to. Liv was great at stuff like this. Perhaps Debs would take her to one side tonight and ask her if she might help her, and maybe even ask about starting to run in the morning too. She couldn't keep putting things off. She was, surprisingly, quite excited about changing her life. If nothing else, she had Eduardo to thank for that.

They walked around the garden, Eduardo pointing out the different plants and flowers. He talked so passionately about them that she realised she had lost her lust for life. She no longer had passion for her job, for her life. Being in a different country with different options was making her realise that she had the power to change things. If she could change her mindset, she felt she could start to change lots of things.

They sat back at the table on the terrace, overlooking the pool and gardens.

'Do you have a family, Deb-orah?' he asked.

'I don't, Eduardo. I did have a husband, but...' She drifted off for a moment and realised it was the first time she'd said that for a while where she didn't feel sad. Perhaps she was starting to realise that you can't get stuck in the past. 'My husband has a new life now and so do I.'

'So what makes you passion? What makes you happy?'

Debs mulled this over.

'I actually don't know the answer to that, Eduardo, but I know that I need to find something.'

'Oh you do, Deb-orah. You *must* find something that makes your heart sing. Something to give you joy in your life. I look at your beautiful face, but you seem so sad at times. I would love to see your eyes sparkle and shine with excitement for life.'

Debs smiled sadly. 'I would love that too. And being here in Portugal is helping me find my sparkle once more, in more ways than you could probably imagine. I do need to think about what I want to do with my life. I used to make things, craft things, and I loved it. but then life took over and I just stopped doing it. Perhaps that's something I could try again, to see if it brings me joy.'

'I would like to see this. You should try it while you are here. What are you doing tomorrow? I would like to take you somewhere, but I would like to keep it a surprise for you.'

'Really? How exciting.' She held her hand to her chest. 'I think the girls were planning to have some golfing lessons.'

'Do you have to go? Or can you come out with me? I would like very much for you to be my, how you say, companion for the day.'

'I would like that very much. I'll check with my friends, as I am here on holiday with them.'

'Where is your phone? Let me give you my number. And then I must go and continue to work.'

Debs reached across to her handbag and retrieved her phone. He took it and entered his number and rang his phone. The shrill ring tone signified that he'd got the call. He saved her number.

'Text me!' He kissed her tenderly on her cheek. 'I have enjoyed today very much. I like to spend time with you. And hopefully, we'll meet tomorrow. Tchau.'

As he disappeared around the side of the villa, through the gardens, she held her hand to her cheek once more, not quite believing that this very handsome man had kissed her again, and wondered whether she was dreaming. She also realised that she hadn't learnt any new words in Portuguese, which was the whole reason he was meant to have popped back to see her.

She went upstairs to her room, and as she passed the large gilt mirror on the landing, she actually stopped, lifted up her chin and took a good look at herself. Her eyes were sparkling, her platinum blonde hair had dried in natural waves which softened her face and her cheeks were pink and flushed. For the first time in a very long time she felt pretty. She never looked at herself in this way. She always felt like a big fat blob with saggy tits and a muffin top. But right now she felt as if she was the most beautiful woman in the world.

She lifted her shoulders and held her head back as she walked into her room. She rummaged through the wardrobe until she found the pretty maxi dress she'd bought at the supermarket but had never thought she'd have the courage to wear. She pulled the dress over her head and smoothed the slinky material down over her backside and her hips. She felt good in it and decided that if the promise of a day out with Eduardo materialised, she would wear this dress.

Chapter Eighteen

DEBS HEARD THE front door fling open and then be slammed shut; a whirlwind of laughter and cheer signifying that the girls were back. She whipped off the maxi dress and shouted that she'd be down in a minute. Once at the bottom of the stairs, she took a deep breath before stepping over the huge number of carrier bags brimming with shopping, which had been abandoned in the hallway, and smiled as she walked into the open-plan lounge area, asking her friends if they'd had a good time.

'We've had a lovely time buying things that we never knew we even needed.' Fiona giggled. 'I haven't had a shopping session like that for years. In fact, the last time was probably when we were in Corfu all those years ago.'

They all laughed.

'Anyone for coffee?' Debs asked.

A chorus of 'yes please' came back and she smiled and went into the kitchen. Liv followed her in.

'You had a good day, Debs? Get up to much?'

Debs blushed and rubbed the back of her neck. 'Nothing much, just hung around the pool.'

'Don't forget I know you, Debs, and I know when you are telling the truth.' She grinned. 'I just wondered why there were two empty cups on the coffee table when there is only one of you.' She raised her eyebrows.

Debs blushed. 'You always were a good detective, Olivia Pemberton. You are wasted as a housewife and mother. You really should have joined the organised crime squad.'

Liv laughed good-naturedly.

Sweeping back into the lounge with a grin on her face, Debs asked, 'So, who bought what and do you still have some money left to go out into Vilamoura later for a meal?'

All the bags were opened and an array of leather goods, sundresses, souvenirs, football shirts and tablecloths were displayed.

'I bet you wished you'd come along now, don't you?'

Debs smiled at Liv, and said, 'I'm sure you had a lovely time, but I've had a really nice day too just chilling out and relaxing here. I am looking forward to going out this evening, though. I hope Vilamoura knows what's going to hit it when these four old slappers hit the streets.'

'Oi, less of the *old* if you don't mind,' shouted Samantha, winking at them as she walked out to the terrace.

EARLY EVENING IN Vilamoura was a bustling hive of activity, with families, couples and beautiful people meandering around the streets, only moving when the roar of a Ferrari or Lamborghini alerted the dawdlers that they needed to get out of the way. The marina was host to fishermen finishing their days out at sea as well as yachts of all sizes, mooring up, the staff of the rich and famous owners ready for an early evening aperitif in one of the bars to start the next stage of the day. The scents of expensive perfume and aftershave permeated the air and mingled with the aroma of the gastronomic delights from the many restaurants scattered around the marina, overlooking the moorings.

They'd seen a restaurant when they'd been into the marina for brunch the previous day that they fancied trying. They were offered the opportunity to sit inside, but after a brief discussion asked if they could sit outside next to the water instead. It seemed a shame to dine inside when they could do that at home. The outside section was buzzing with life, families dining together, couples holding hands, friends chatting and laughing, the chilled-out holiday vibe making it feel a relaxed and perfect setting for their evening meal. They were shown to an inviting candle-lit, beautifully laid table, next to the water's edge.

The waiter brought olives, bread and tuna paste to their table, along with a bottle of still and a bottle of sparkling water and gave out menus. The ladies oohed and aahed then asked for a little more time to choose what they wanted. They had all made their decisions except for Debs. So much choice confused her, but remembering her decision earlier to be healthier, she settled on salmon, crushed potatoes and sautéed vegetables.

Liv raised her eyebrows at Debs when she'd made her choice. It was most unlike her to have a meal without chips. Liv made a note to take her to one side later for a chat. There was a sparkle in her eyes that wasn't there last night, and Liv wondered just what she had been up to today that she wasn't telling them about.

'I'm so looking forward to our golf lesson to-morrow. Are you, Debs?' she asked.

'Erm, well... I was going to chat to you about that, actually. Would you mind awfully if I didn't come along?' She held her hand to her neck and Liv saw her skin turning pink.

'Had a better offer, have you?' said Samantha with a laugh.

This time Debs went full-on beetroot red. 'Actually, yes, I have.'

'My goodness, Debs, you're a dark horse. I think you'd better tell us what's been going on,' said Samantha.

Debs took a deep breath. 'Well...'

'Ladies, good evening.' They looked up at the familiar voice and saw Mikey walking by with an older couple, who they presumed must be his parents. Mikey introduced them all. It was only when his father Keith called him *Michael*, that Liv remembered that he'd asked them to call him that in front of his parents.

Debs seemed really glad of the diversion and with excitement in her voice, invited Mikey and his parents to join them.

'No, it's fine really, thank you. Very kind, but thank you.' Mikey looked horrified at the thought.

'Oh what a lovely idea, Michael. Thank you, ladies, we'd love to join you. Wouldn't we, Angela?'

Mikey's mum nodded enthusiastically, and Liv called the waiter back over and asked if they could add a table to theirs so that they could all sit together. Mikey was as white as a sheet but sat down all the same.

His mother finally spoke. 'It would be lovely to get to know our villa neighbours. Michael has been telling us all about you.' She stroked his hair as if he was still a child.

Mikey pulled away, batting her hand. 'Please excuse my mum. She still thinks I'm ten, despite the fact that I'm a grown man.'

She laughed good-naturedly at him and he smiled back at her.

'I don't get to see you very often and you'll always be my baby boy no matter how old you are.'

Mikey shook his head and laughed. 'Mum, I'm twenty-seven!'

'And how's that boss of yours? Bernardo, isn't it?' his father asked. 'You've not said much about him.'

Mikey fidgeted in his seat. 'Erm, yes, he's fine, thanks. Business is going well for the time of year so he's happy.'

'That's good. He should be happy having someone like you working for him. I bet his wife is a looker, he's a very handsome man. It's so nice of them to let you rent a spare room from them.'

Mikey quickly changed the subject and asked

the ladies what their plans were for the rest of their holiday.

'Well, one of the nights we'd like to see if we can have a sunset tour on a yacht, if we can arrange it. I was going to see if you had any contacts. I've got the name and number of one that we saw,' said Liv.

'You can definitely leave that one with me. I know just the company to sort that out for you. In fact, that's one of their fabulous boats over there. That big white one on the end.' There were lots of appreciative noises from around the table. 'I'll sort that out first thing in the morning and give you a bell, Olivia.'

'That's perfect. I think it's actually the one that we saw earlier. Thank you. That would be wonderful. You really are a darling, you know. And then we're going to go to the casino tomorrow night and try our hand at winning a fortune.'

'Ooh how exciting.' Angela clapped her hands in quick succession. 'I do love a little flutter!'

'Why don't you all come with us?' Liv's mouth spoke the words before her brain had engaged. She looked over at Mikey, who was trying discreetly to shake his head. She immediately knew that she'd made a huge mistake. One that could not now be undone.

'Oh yes, how wonderful. That would be fabulous, wouldn't it, darling? Oh Michael, why don't you ask Bernardo to join us too. It would be a great opportunity to get to know your boss a little better. Go on, message him now.'

Mikey closed his eyes but only Liv seemed to sense that he was extremely uncomfortable. His father could be quite assertive when he wanted.

Keith wouldn't give up on the Bernardo situation and insisted that Mikey either rang him or sent him a text to invite him to the casino the following evening. He had no alternative but to do as his father had told him to.

He did, however, loosen up over dinner and relaxed into the evening and appeared to be enjoying spending time with his parents. The girls were all on their best behaviour and everyone got on famously. They talked about how much they were looking forward to their golf lessons the following day, which Mikey had arranged.

'You are *so* going to adore the professional that I've got giving lessons tomorrow.' He clapped his hands together excitedly.

'Debs isn't coming though. However, she won't tell us what she's doing instead. Perhaps you can get it out of her Mikeea—Ouch.' Liv had kicked Fiona under the table.

'Do tell, Debs. Have you got yourself a Portuguese lover to take you out for the day?' asked Mikey.

Debs flushed scarlet and squirmed in her seat.

'Oh! My! God! You have too, you little minx!' he squealed, then covered his mouth and started coughing, probably realising, Liv guessed, how camp he had sounded.

Debs, after lots of interrogation, confessed she'd been invited out with Eduardo on his day off.

'Now that is a turn up for the books. Eduardo hasn't had a girlfriend for a while according to Josep. How exciting. I can't wait to hear all about it,' said Mikey.

'Well, maybe not *all* about it, eh, Debs?' Keith nudged Debs' elbow and she buried her head in her hands looking totally mortified.

'Well, I hope you have a lovely day. You deserve a bit of happiness and I can see that he makes you smile and that's all you can ask for in life really, isn't it? Good for you, Debs.' Liv smiled kindly at her friend, hoping genuinely that she'd have a nice day out but also hoping she wouldn't get too involved. Where could it possibly go, when they lived in different countries? But a bit of fun while they were here would be really good for Debs' spirit.

THEY HAD A wonderful evening out, Mikey's parents were really good company, and at the end of the evening, when the yawns started to become obvious, Mikey arranged for two cars to pick them all up and take them home. They made arrangements to meet up at the entrance to the casino the following evening.

Once back at the villa, Liv asked if anyone wanted a nightcap before bed, and laughed when Fiona asked if they'd think her a stick in the mud if she'd rather have a cup of tea. They all laughed and the other three agreed that they'd also rather have a cup of tea. Liv thought that Debs would probably have a drink, but even she said that she'd prefer a cuppa.

Liv knew there was more of a sparkle in Debs' eye than there was last night, and she was dying for Debs to dish the dirt on her and Eduardo, but she knew that it had to be in her own time. This evening, when anyone asked her what she'd done that day, she'd got a little flustered, stuttered over her words and gone bright red in the face. And it wasn't a sun-kissed flush in the face, or a menopausal one. It was definitely the first flush of excitement because a man that she liked was giving her some attention. And she deserved it so much.

Even if nothing ever came of it, she loved that she was feeling the fluttering of attraction.

AS DEBS GOT into bed and pulled the sheet up around her shoulders, her phoned pinged.

Hope tomorrow is still OK, Deborah. I pick you up at ten thirty if I don't hear from you.

Her heart skipped a beat. Those butterflies fluttered again in her tummy.

Looking forward to it. Goodnight x

Not as much as me. Goodnight beautiful lady. Sweet dreams xx

She felt ridiculously excited. She wondered how on earth she was supposed to sleep.

WHEN MIKEY ARRIVED back at his swanky apartment, which overlooked the marina, Bernardo was sitting on the sofa, swirling a small amount of liquid around in the bottom of a brandy glass.

'So, you've told them about us then?' he asked Mikey.

Mikey took the glass from his hand and placed it on the table. He held Bernardo's hands in his.

'Well, not exactly. There just wasn't the opportunity this evening. I'm sorry.'

'Not as sorry as I am, Mikey.' Bernardo took his hands away. He stroked a finger down Mikey's arm. 'I love you more than you will ever know. But we cannot go on like this any more. If you don't tell them by the end of tomorrow night, then we're over, Mikey.'

He reached across and kissed Mikey's cheek, walked into their bedroom and shut the door.

Mikey's chin trembled and a tear escaped. He was torn between upsetting his parents and risking them wanting nothing more to do with him, and losing the man he loved with all of his heart. What a decision to have to make. But it sounded like he needed to make his choice in the next twenty-four hours. He pulled a cashmere throw, which had been artistically draped across the back of the sofa, over himself, curled his knees up to his chest and silently cried himself to sleep.

Chapter Nineteen

LIV GROANED AS she rolled over and looked at the bedside clock. Eight a.m. She slept like a log out here. At home she was normally up at six a.m., trying to grab a cup of coffee in peace, to wake up gently, before sorting out the family and going through the morning ritual of everyone shouting, 'Mum!' or 'Olivia, where's my…?' Once they were all packed off to school and work, she'd heave a sigh of relief and grab Hector's lead. Once he heard that familiar jangle, he'd come running from wherever he was in the house – he had super hearing for things like that. They'd jump in the car and go to the forest, which was literally just at the end of their long country road.

It did her good to get away from the house; it oppressed her at times. Sometimes they ran, sometimes they walked, depending on her mood. There were times when she just needed the pace to slow, so a walk amongst the trees was therapeutic and calmed her down. There was something about being surrounded by trees. She wasn't a tree hugger, but she definitely felt a benefit from being in the forest, she felt grounded and at peace. Just her and Hector, the odd mountain biker and other dog walkers. She missed Hector.

She did not miss the hectic mornings. Even the weekends were full-on these days, with football on a Saturday morning for one son and rugby on a Sunday morning for the other. And George played golf most weekends on both days, so it was all left to her and she'd be expected to drop him off then wait for his call to say he wanted a lift home, at whatever that time may be. She could never entirely relax. It would have been nice some weekends to pour herself a glass of wine and chill out in front of the TV, but she'd learnt a long time ago that she'd always be expected to drop everything to chauffeur one of the males in her life somewhere.

Sometimes she just wanted life to slow down so she could take stock of what she wanted. She was unhappy, but she wasn't sure what being happy looked like any more.

Before they'd had children, she and George used to love their Saturday nights in, snuggling up on the sofa together, watching a film with a cheap bottle of wine and fish and chips. Now, on a Saturday evening, if he wasn't at the golf club, there was nearly always some function they had to go to, a charity event that George wanted to be seen at because it was good for his business connections.

He'd changed so much. 'Family first' used to be his motto. Now it was always the business that came ahead of everyone and everything, and she was left to deal with all the family stuff. She knew that lots of people would love to be in her position. She didn't have to work, had access to as much money as she wanted, had loads of time on her hands while the kids were at school, so she could have been a lady who lunches, or spent every day shopping if she wanted to. Some of her friends were amazed that even though she didn't work, George allowed her to have a cleaner, but their house was so huge, she'd never be able to keep on top of it without some help.

So, yes, in theory, she had a nice life. But she'd lost her spirit. She'd lost her purpose. She missed their old life very much and would swap it back in a heartbeat.

HER PLAN FOR today had been to get up early, go for a run and be back by now, but she was on holiday, after all, and did she really want to go for a run?

But she knew that not going today would mean

that she probably wouldn't go for the rest of the time she was in Vilamoura. Running for her was a daily habit – if broken, she might not be able to get back into the rhythm of it.

Her running clothes were placed over the armchair in the corner of the room, so she popped to the loo in the en suite, brushed her teeth and tied her hair back, then got dressed. As she crept out of her room, closing the door behind her, she didn't think anyone was up. She tiptoed down the stairs and started doing some stretching exercises on the bottom couple of steps.

'Can you help me to run, Liv?'

Liv clutched her chest. 'Jeez, Debs! You scared the life out of me. What are you doing creeping up behind me and lurking around in the hallway?'

'Sorry, lovely. I didn't mean to scare you. I wondered whether you might sit down with me later and put a plan together for me to start running. I really want to lose some weight, Liv, and I've made up my mind that I'm going to start to run.'

'That's brilliant, Debs. Go grab the spare pair of running shoes that are in my wardrobe and come with me now.'

'Oh no. I'll only hold you up.'

'Come on, Debs, I really don't mind. And I'd

love to help you. We can do a bit of running and a bit of fast walking. Honestly, go grab my running shoes and we'll go now. No time like the present. Go now, before you change your mind.'

DEBS WAS OUT of breath before she got to the top of the stairs, never mind after any running. She'd probably have a heart attack before she got to the top of the street. She didn't want to let Liv down, though, and she needed help because she clearly couldn't do it on her own.

Liv gave her some stretches to do when she came down the stairs and then opened the door.

'Here.' Liv threw a bottle of water at her. 'Come on. Let's go. This time tomorrow, you'll be so glad you did it today. And I'm so blooming proud of you for trying.'

That was all Debs needed to hear to motivate her. It had been literally years since she remembered anyone saying that they were proud of her. Liv jogged on the spot while Debs closed the gate behind her, and they set off walking down the small cul-de-sac at a brisk pace.

'Right, we're going to do a small run now,' said Liv. 'You see that tree at the bottom of the road? We're going to run to that.'

'Shit, Liv, that looks miles away.'

Liv laughed. 'It's about five hundred yards. And you are just going to do a gentle run. Nothing more. I think you'll surprise yourself.'

They started to jog.

'You need to remember to breathe, Debs.' Liv laughed, but she was right. Debs was literally holding her breath. 'I always remember that about you at uni. When you went swimming you used to hold your breath from one end of the pool to the other. You must remember the breathing. Once you get your breathing right it'll make life so much easier. Inhale deep breaths through your nose, and exhale through your mouth.'

Debs knew that Liv knew what she was talking about, and Debs knew that she needed to take notice of Liv. There was no point doing it her way. She didn't know best, even though in the past she thought she did. She needed Liv to help her and would do everything she told her to.

Before she knew it, they were at the tree.

'OMG! I. Did. It!' she wheezed.

Liv high-fived her. 'You did. Well done. Now let's power walk for a bit and then we'll find another marker and run again.'

'Are you sure I'm not ruining your running time, Liv? I do feel bad.'

'I feel really good to be helping you, matey, so please don't worry. Let me help. It's nice to have someone depend on me for different reasons than my family do.'

'Is everything OK at home, Liv? You've made a few comments this week that make me feel otherwise.'

'Nothing that a few days away won't cure, I'm sure. I'll talk about it when I'm ready, Debs, I promise. But right now, I don't want you to think about talking. I just want you to focus on your breathing. Now, you see that supermarket on the corner up ahead? We're going to run to that.'

'OK, let's go!'

DEBS WAS A perfect student. It made Liv feel great to help her. She loved being able to help people. It made her feel valuable. At home, she just felt used, not needed for being her. Just needed because they relied on her. She felt free here, free from being responsible for others, but also guilty because she was enjoying having some space to herself, some time to free up her head and think about other things than her family. She felt bad because she was *really* enjoying it.

'I'M SO BLOODY proud of you, Debs. I really am.'

'I'm feeling pretty proud of myself right now. I can't believe I did that.'

'You did so well. You're not as unfit as you thought you were. Each day, you can do a bit more and keep building, until eventually you'll be doing more running than walking and there'll be no stopping you.'

'And it's so much easier when you breathe too.'

They both laughed as they walked through the front door. Samantha was just walking through to the lounge area and looked most surprised to see Debs with Liv.

'I'm helping Debs start to run,' Liv explained.

'Good for you, Debs,' Samantha replied. 'You should do that for a living, Liv. I bet you are very motivating. I know some personal trainers are all shouty and sergeant-major like, but that would piss me right off and I'd probably end up thumping the person who shouted at me.'

'Well, I know it's only my first time today, but I've made a start and it felt good. And you're right, Samantha, Liv is really patient and encouraging. You *should* think about doing it for a job, Liv. You could really help people to transform themselves. You'd be brilliant.'

'That's really nice of you to say so, ladies, but I

think you're overselling me. I'm nowhere near good enough to teach people. Might be something to think about, though. I could train to do something like that. I'm going up for a shower, see you in a bit. I'm starving now. Ready for breakfast.'

As Liv slathered herself in her Jo Malone English Pear and Freesia shower gel that she'd treated herself to at the airport, she mulled over what Samantha and Debs had said. Perhaps there was something in it. She loved to help people. She'd always loved helping people to choose clothes too, when that had been her job. Perhaps she could help people transform themselves. Maybe she could mix being a helping hand to someone to keep fit or lose weight, or both, with helping them revive their wardrobes or make shopping decisions. The more she thought about it, the more she liked it. She'd run it by the girls over breakfast and see if they had any bright ideas.

And, oh boy, did they have ideas! Over endless cups of freshly ground coffee, warm croissants and fresh fruit and yoghurt, her friends inspired her further. Fiona suggested that Liv became a personal shopper and set up a Facebook page advising people on style and putting different outfits together. Samantha suggested that she also set up a blog and looked at getting sponsorship from clothes companies. Debs suggested that she might be able to team up with a make-up artist and teach people how to have a new look. Liv also tested out the idea that she could work with Mikey, doing inspirational holiday breaks, maybe even in Portugal. That idea got a huge 'ooh' from them all and they volunteered to be her first clients.

Between the four of them, they'd got Liv's mind working overtime. She was excited and energised. She hadn't felt like this for a very long time. And it felt really good.

Liv sat back and looked at these women who she'd known for over thirty years. They'd lost a little of their friendship over the decades, as their lives moved in different directions, but they had never lost touch totally and were always there for each other. She knew that if she hadn't spoken to any of them for months, then rang them up at three a.m. and said she needed them right then, they would be there without fail. Friends like that were priceless. Friends that you knew you could rely on no matter what.

She hoped that they would all return from this break in Portugal feeling lighter and more at ease with the world. A wonderful thing happened when you put strong women together. They lifted and inspired each other. They motivated and encouraged each other. They supported and spurred you on to do better and to be the best version of yourself that you could be. This is how she'd felt when they were friends at uni and in their younger lives. And this was exactly how she felt right now. She was so glad she had invited them along on this holiday. She didn't think they'd ever realise just how much she needed their friendship at this stage of her life and how much this holiday might already have made a big difference to her and how she felt.

Chapter Twenty

'CAR'S HERE!' LIV yelled from the hallway.

Fiona and Samantha came bounding down the stairs. 'Are you sure you don't want to come, Debs? Sure you'd rather spend the day with Eduardo than us?' They giggled.

'Erm, let me think about that for a moment?' Debs grinned mischievously. 'Are you sure you don't mind really, girls?'

'God, if I had the chance to spend the day with a gorgeous man with a sexy bum and a Portuguese accent or go out with you lot for the day, I know what I'd be choosing. Adeus, meus amigos!' Samantha put on a sun visor, looking quite the golfing part in her navy pedal pushers, white vest top and white pumps.

'Don't do anything we wouldn't,' Fiona shouted, followed by a very dirty laugh.

Liv touched her arm. 'Have a great day, darling. See you later.'

A KNOCK AT the door made Debs catch her breath and she took one last look at herself in the bedroom mirror. This was becoming a habit, that was twice now in as many days. Maybe mirrors weren't her nemesis after all. Maybe *she* was her own worst enemy. She turned this way and that and decided that she looked quite nice. Her hair had dried naturally, so it was wavy and softly feminine, looking a little blonder from the sun. Her face was definitely looking more sun-kissed than when she arrived, but the main difference was that she couldn't stop smiling.

She slipped her feet into her sparkly flip-flops, scooped up the bottom of her maxi dress in her hand and skittered down the stairway. As she pulled open the door, Eduardo was standing down the path, leaning up against a shiny red-and-silver moped. She threw her head back and laughed out loud. 'And you expect me to go on that, in this dress? Shall I go and change?'

Without breaking eye contact, Eduardo walked towards her, only stopping when he was so close that she could feel his soft breath on her face, and she could smell the musky tones of his aftershave. Her lips parted and she let out a sigh. It was if she had physically swooned like in the old movies.

'You are perfect, just as you are, Debs. We will

manage.' He kissed her cheek tenderly and held out his hand to her, which she took. 'Although I am sorry, but you will have to wear a helmet over your pretty hair,' he said.

She closed the door behind her and they walked down the garden path to the moped. He tucked a strand of hair behind her ear and as he touched her skin, she shivered.

'You will have to put your arms around me and hold me tight.'

Debs grinned. 'I'm sure I can manage that!'

He handed her a white helmet and he shook it gently to make sure it was on safely and fastened it at her chin. All the while, he didn't take his eyes from hers. Bloody hell. He was beautiful and she was mesmerised by his piercing eyes. He put his helmet on, gave her a wink and they both mounted the bike. There was something incredibly sexy about sitting so close to this man and wrapping her thighs around his.

'OK, hold me tight! We will not go fast though. I promise I take care of you.'

She slid her arms around his waist and pressed her breasts up against his back. She was glad that she'd thought to put her denim jacket on, so he couldn't feel her nipples harden through the fabric. She told herself to calm down but couldn't stop giggling and wondered what the girls would say if they could see her now.

Twenty minutes later, they arrived at an out-of-town shopping area. Eduardo dismounted and steadied her as she alighted the moped and stretched her legs. He helped her to take off her helmet and she shook out her hair. Luckily, helmet hair suited her natural waves; she was glad she hadn't spent ages straightening it this morning.

'You OK?' he enquired.

She still couldn't stop smiling and nodded.

He took her arm and folded it into his and they walked towards a row of shops. She had no idea where they were going but they headed towards a shop called Crafty Cockney. Through the window, she could see someone sitting at a sewing machine and wondered what sort of shop it was. She was still none the wiser until they walked through the door and she saw a huge shelf stacked high with colourful arts and craft materials.

'Alright, Eddie darling, how are you? Haven't seen you for a while. What brings you here today?' A larger-than-life lady, with a heavy London accent and bright-red hair which matched her lipstick perfectly, greeted Eduardo by kissing him on both cheeks.

'This is my good friend, Debs. She likes to do

the crafts, but she has nothing here with her, so I bring her to you, Margo, to help her to get some basic things for her to make a start.'

'Oh, Eduardo.' Debs put her hand on her heart. 'That's so kind of you.'

He brushed her cheek with his lips. 'I will be back in half one hour. Margo, may I just have a word outside, please?'

'Have a look round, me darling. I'll be back in a jiffy.'

Debs had always been a tactile person and couldn't help stroking the rolls of colourful cotton and stunning silk fabric as she glided her hand along the shelves which were full to bursting. Other shelves held millions of different coloured balls of wool, with every sized knitting needle and crochet hook that you could possibly ever need, to racks and racks of paper for crafting, knitting and crochet patterns, sewing kits and cross-stitch patterns. This was a real treasure trove, there were so many glorious things in this shop, she didn't know where to look first.

She was in a little world of her own when Margo came back into the shop. 'Alright, sweets?'

'Oh, Margo, what a wonderful shop. Is it yours?'

'It sure is, been here for over ten years.'

'It's just fabulous. Have you lived in Portugal for long?'

'I came out on holiday once twenty-five years ago and had a holiday romance. Went back to London and missed the bare bones of him. I had a shitty job in a factory, which I hated. So I took a gamble and prayed to the gods that he felt the same. We didn't have mobile phones in those days to keep in touch like we do now. I packed my job in, sold everything I had, booked a one-way ticket and I've never been back.'

'Goodness me. What a story.'

'Well, I always think you have to look back and regret the things you've done, rather than regret the things you haven't done. I might have wondered for all of my life if I should have done it, if I hadn't.'

'Wow! It's so brave, though. So you've been together since then?'

'No, he turned out to be a total wanker, and after about three weeks I couldn't stand the sight of him, so I dumped him and shacked up with his best mate instead.' Her face lit up as she grinned widely, and Debs realised how much she liked her warm openness and total honesty, even when she'd only just met her. 'Josep and I have been married for eighteen years and we have two children. He's a chef. And he still makes my heart sing. Oh and he's Eduardo's brother.'

'Ah! So your Josep is the handsome man who cooked our dinner the other evening. Wow. It's such a small world.'

'Ah, it's all making sense now. Pep, I call him, did come home and say that he'd met four glamorous ladies up at one of the big villas on the hill that overlooked the sea. How funny. Now Eduardo, he doesn't often have lady friends. Don't tell him I told you this, but he had his heart broken a long time ago and has never really bothered with women since. But the way he looks at you, it's different. I can tell that he likes you very much. He lights up around you.'

Debs fiddled with the cuff on her denim jacket and her cheeks flushed. 'I like him too. I *really* like him.'

'How wonderful. Let's have a cuppa and we can chat more before he comes back. I'll text him and tell him to be a bit longer. Anyway, he's also just paid me one hundred Euros and said you need to choose some craft materials.'

'I can't let him do that. That's way too generous of him.'

'Oh let him, darling, he's got no one else to spend his money on. There's something to be said for not having loads of kids, you know. Bloody leeches.' She winked as she walked to the corner of the shop and turned to fill the kettle in the sink.

Pinned to the wall was a list of craft workshops Margo ran in the shop, and Debs wished with all her heart she was staying longer. She would have loved to come to some of the pottery painting. It was something she'd always wanted to do and never got around to trying. There were some sewing workshops that she'd have loved to do too. She made a mental note to make sure that when she got home she looked up some similar places she could go to. She felt excited about getting involved in craft-making again. It surprised her that she'd forgotten how much she used to enjoy spending her weekends doing arts and crafts and also how good she was at it.

They chatted as if they'd known each other for years, and Debs felt Margo was someone who, in different circumstances, she would have loved to be good friends with. She felt a shiver, and when she glanced up, Eduardo was looking at her through the window. He was so handsome and when he smiled at her, her heart flipped every time. Debs still couldn't believe that he had brought her here today and treated her to a shopping spree. Dave would never have done anything like this. He always thought she was wasting time if she sat and did something crafty at home. It was OK for him to sit and watch football on the TV for hours on end, but he seemed to hate her sitting and doing something which she loved and which she found relaxing too. It was so hard at one point, because she'd get out her craft stuff and put it on the dining-room table where she was working and Dave would throw it all into a cardboard box, messing everything up.

He certainly never respected anything she was doing. She didn't know Eduardo well, but she had the feeling that he would always treat her with respect. It was such a shame that in a few days she'd be flying home. She couldn't help but wish that things were different. But she wasn't going to spoil this precious and wonderful time by wishing it away. She was determined she was going to make the most of every single minute.

Eduardo was so considerate that he'd even thought to bring a rucksack with him, so Debs could pack the things she'd bought in the bag on the journey back. As Margo waved them off from the doorway of Debs' new favourite shop, literally in the whole world, she snuggled into Eduardo's back, her arms around his waist. He reached behind and squeezed her arm. She felt that this man could protect her from anything.

They arrived back at the villa just after one p.m.

'Will you stay for lunch, Eduardo?'

'I would like that very much.'

Debs threw together a salad and some cold meats with some more of the delicious fresh bread that was left on the doorstep every morning by the local baker. They chatted comfortably over lunch, the language difference not being a barrier in any way whatsoever. She asked him to teach her some more Portuguese words. She could listen to that accent all day long. She was quite sure that if he read out a shopping list in his sexy voice, she'd melt.

'Eu gosto muito de você.'

'What does that mean?'

'It means, "I like you very much."'

Debs blushed. 'I like you very much too.'

Moving closer to her, he took her hand, intertwining their fingers. Her heart began to beat faster and her body tingled from head to toe. God, what was this man doing to her. She was reduced to feeling like a fifteen-year-old with her first crush and it felt uncontrollable.

His head bent towards her and he kissed the tip of her nose. His touch was as light as a feather. She was sure he could feel her body trembling. She didn't know whether it was with nerves, fear, excitement or anticipation, but it felt as if her heart was pounding loud enough for him to hear.

His warm soft lips touched hers so gently and hers melted against them. His tongue flicked across her bottom lip so delicately, she wondered whether she'd imagined it. And then the gentleness got a whole lot more passionate.

Chapter Twenty-One

DEBS' HEART BEGAN to beat faster. Eduardo moved his head away from hers and it felt as if her lips were on fire. His soft stubbly beard had awoken a million nerve endings and her chin was tingling.

'Do you believe in fate, Debs?' His eyes bored into hers.

She nodded, unable to speak.

'Do you believe that some people are meant to be together even though they've only just met? How do you call it in England? First sight love?'

She nodded. 'Love at first sight, yes.'

'I do too, Debs.'

He turned towards her and gently stroked her breast at the same time as biting her bottom lip. A moan escaped from her lips.

'Quero fazer amor com você.'

She was pretty sure that even if he said, 'I'm just going to put the bins out' it would tickle her ovaries.

She whispered, 'What does that mean?'

'It means, I want to make love to you right now.'

'Oh!' Her mind was working overtime. Shit, shit, shit.

'Would you like that too?'

She hesitated. She wondered what the hell she was doing sitting here in a passionate embrace with a man who two days ago she didn't even know. It seemed like the maddest thing in the world, yet the most right thing at the very same time. She recalled what Margo had said earlier: it was better to look back and regret the things you'd done, than look back and wished that you'd done them. And right now, she wanted this man so much. She smiled at Eduardo and nodded her agreement.

He swooped down and lifted her up and carried her through to the lounge, laying her on the sofa. He started to undress her. Grabbing the throw that was draped across the back of the sofa, she tried to cover herself, but he took it away and took the rest of her clothes off until she lay on the sofa totally naked.

'You are beautiful, I want to see all of you.'

Working his way up her body from her toes, he laid featherlight kisses all the way to her fingertips.

She thought her body might explode, and that was before he gently eased himself inside her and took her to a place of ecstasy that she'd *never* been before.

'DEBS, YOU ARE amazing. How have I only just met you? I feel like I know you forever.'

He wrapped the cashmere throw tenderly around her shoulders and slowly ran his finger down her thigh, before he stretched and stood, starting to get dressed. She sighed. She really couldn't believe that this bronzed, half-naked, gorgeous man standing before her had wanted her and that she'd just had sex with him.

She'd never slept with another man. Dave had been her boyfriend from the age of fifteen. They lost their virginity together on her sixteenth birthday and he had been the only man she'd ever slept with. Sex with Dave had turned into more of a chore by the end. Something you knew you had to do and did as quickly as you could because you had lots of other jobs to get on with. In complete contrast, being with Eduardo was the most sensual, erotic experience she'd ever had and it had felt so right.

Eduardo looked at his watch.

'Do you have to go?' she asked, feeling quite needy at that moment. This had been an absolutely huge step for her and she hoped it wasn't going to be something that she quickly regretted.

'Not right now, but I will have to go soon. Besides, your friends might be back.'

She nodded. 'Can you stay for a tiny bit longer?'

'Of course, my love. But then I must go and water the gardens in this area before the sun dries them out.'

Debs sincerely hoped that gardens would be the only thing he would be tending to in the other three properties. An awful thought popped into her mind. Perhaps this is what Eduardo did. Perhaps he was a complete and utter tart, who preyed on women on holiday, got what he wanted from them, and then never saw them again. She became hot and flustered, wondering if all those lovely words he'd said to her might be lies and if she'd been well and truly taken in by them. What a fool she would feel if she found that out.

As if reading her mind, Eduardo sat by her side and reached for her hands, leaning against her.

'Debs, I want to know everything about you. I want to be with you more. I want you to know that I think you are most beautiful lady I meet. And I want you to know that I don't do this, with anyone before. It has been a long time since I feel this way about a woman.'

She stood and picked up her clothes, throwing her dress over her head and retrieving her pants from the floor. Thank goodness she'd thought to put a decent pair on today, just in case, and hadn't worn the frumpy, comfy old granny ones she normally wore.

'But, Eduardo, I'm fat and old and—'

He held his finger up to her lips. 'Shhhh! You are most beautiful to me, Debs. I wish I could make you see what I can see. I see a very sexy lady with gorgeous curves. I see a woman with a smile that lights up a room. I see a woman who has seen life and knows about the world. And I see a lady who I cannot stop thinking about, and who makes my heart beat hard.' He banged his fist on his chest. 'You make me smile and be happy than I have ever been, and I want to be with you.' He reached down and kissed her slowly and gently on the lips and she felt like she was just melting. Goodness, what was happening to her?

'Would it be too much if I asked you to come out with me again tomorrow? Would your friends mind if you left them for another day? I would like to show you more of my beautiful country and if you would allow me, I would like to show you my home.'

Debs thought she was dreaming. She couldn't understand why he believed those things and wanted to spend time with her. She wondered whether the girls would be mad with her if she spent yet another day apart from them. After all, this was supposed to be their holiday for spending time together. But, she couldn't help herself and she nodded at him.

'I'd love to.'

He opened his arms and she snuggled against his warm body, and it felt as if they fitted together perfectly.

'I have only been in love once, Debs, and it was a long time ago. I don't remember ever feeling like this though. What about you?'

'I was married for a long time, but then Dave, my husband, he fell out of love with me and into love with someone else. Someone younger and prettier, and thinner and a real blonde.'

'And how do you feel about this?'

'Well, at first it was a huge shock. I never saw it coming, but I suppose I'm getting used to doing things on my own now. This trip to Portugal is the first time I've ever flown alone in nearly fifty years.'

'Oh my God! You are telling me that you are nearly fifty. Never.' He feigned shock.

She tapped his arm playfully and grinned. 'In my head I'm only about twenty-three, but everything else tells me I'm at least fifty. How old are you, Eduardo?'

'I'm forty-five. So I can be your Portuguese toy? Is that how they say it in England? You are my leopard.'

Debs giggled. 'Toy boy. And cougar. But close enough.' She never thought she'd ever use those words in relation to herself. 'Does it not bother you that I'm older than you?'

He shrugged. 'Why would it?'

She loved the way he looked at life. Nothing seemed to faze him. Perhaps that's what living in the sun and doing a job that you love does for you. Dave was constantly moaning about how he hated his job at an engineering company. She'd told him many times to find something else, or to retrain, but he couldn't motivate himself to do anything about it and seemed to prefer that he had something to moan about. She couldn't help but compare the two men. They were so incredibly different.

'I will message you later,' Eduardo said, interrupting her thoughts. 'Até amanhã, meu amor.' He kissed her hand and walked away.

The minute he'd gone, she missed his presence.

She couldn't believe that he'd made such an impression on her in such a short time.

DEBS WAS AT the dining table, enjoying experimenting with some of the craft stuff that she'd bought, when the others arrived. She'd needed something to keep her mind busy, because since Eduardo had left, it had been working overtime.

'Yoohoo! We're back!'

Debs looked up and smiled at her friends, and Liv wandered over to the table to see what she was doing.

'I'm sure when you're ready you'll tell us what has been going on here that has put a dirty great smile on your face. Because I'm sure that crafting alone won't have done that. Fancy a coffee?' She winked at Debs and walked into the kitchen, then back into the lounge a few minutes later, carrying a tray of mugs.

Debs couldn't look Liv in the eye as she wandered over to the sofa, picked up and folded the cashmere throw and smoothed the sofa over, saying that she'd had a little sleep as she hadn't slept well last night. Out of the corner of her eye, she could see Liv smirking and she felt like giggling. She felt on top of the world and she'd always be grateful to Eduardo for making her feel this way. She felt a million dollars and had started to believe that perhaps she was all those things that he said. Instead of feeling fat and frumpy, she felt voluptuous and sexy. She'd never felt this way before and she liked this new her.

'Anyway, tell me about your golf lesson,' Debs said. 'Was it good? Did you have a handsome golf teacher?'

'It was really good,' said Samantha. 'We spent some time on the range just shooting some balls.' Debs tittered at that expression, and Samantha tutted at her playfully before continuing. 'Then we went onto the green. We all had a good go and I don't think we embarrassed ourselves too much, did we, girls?'

'I really enjoyed it. But then out here it would be good. The sun is shining and it's roasting. I still don't see the attraction when you are in England and it's chucking it down with rain,' said Liv. 'Yet George still seems to love it. Probably because he gets to have an afternoon without the boys and me screaming at each other.'

Samantha added, 'I tell you what though, Debs, you should take up golf if you're looking for a bloke. It's a great way to meet men, and all they want to do is make themselves look good so they're happy to teach. And it's quite nice. I have to say, when a man is snuggling into your bottom from behind, with his arms wrapped around you, trying to teach you how to swing a club. I kept pretending I didn't get it, just so I could carry on in that position. I think he must have had a gun in his pocket though!'

They all laughed at Samantha.

'It made me feel like getting a bloke of my own. Perhaps that's something to look into when I get back. Perhaps I need to enrol at a local golf course,' she said.

'Oh, I forgot to tell you, Debs. We've booked a boat trip. Mikey got in touch with the company we'd seen – remember those two gorgeous men? – and we're going on a sunset sail tomorrow evening. It's going to be fab,' said Liv.

'Brilliant. That sounds delightful,' said Debs, hoping she'd be back in time from her day out.

'And don't think for one minute you're not going to tell us all about what you've been up to today either, lady,' said Liv.

Fiona clearly hadn't nodded off like Debs thought she had, even though she was looking awfully comfy on the reclining chair. She lifted one eyelid and said, 'There are some bits I think she probably *shouldn't* tell us about.'

More laughs followed and Debs told them about meeting Margo at the craft shop and how she'd loved whiling away a couple of hours making cards and bookmarks and she showed off her creations to lots of oohs and aahs.

'They're so good, Debs, you should start selling them.' Samantha picked up the craft items and turned them over, nodding approvingly.

'Ah, it's just something I like doing. It helps me to relax.'

'Well, I have loads of birthdays coming up over the next few months,' Liv excitedly mentioned. 'I'd love you to make some cards for me to give and maybe some little gifts too. What do you think, Debs?'

Debs smiled and knew that she would really love to take on a few commissions to get her back into the swing of things. Who knew? Maybe when she got home she'd find out where the local craft fayres were held and maybe have a small stand and see what the interest was. But then a wave of sadness hit her as the thought about going home, realising she'd be leaving a little bit of herself behind here in Portugal.

She'd been obsessively checking her phone every five minutes before the girls got back, wondering whether she would hear from Eduardo about the day out he had promised her. But since they'd got back she'd been busy so she was surprised when her phone pinged.

> *My beautiful Debs. I will pick you up at ten a.m. Bernardo tells me that there is a boat trip for you ladies tomorrow night, so I will have you back in time. Have a wonderful evening with your friends. E x*

Her heart skipped a beat and as she looked up she saw Liv and that smirk again, and she grinned back at her.

'Well, I don't know about you guys but I'm going to have a soak in the bath and get myself glammed up for this evening. I'm so looking forward to this casino night.'

Debs left the room with some swagger to her walk.

Chapter Twenty-Two

'WHOA! THAT'S IMPRESSIVE.' Debs was dazzled by the exterior of the casino before she'd even stepped out of the car. The limo circled the central courtyard's lit-up multi-coloured fountain, pulling up to a gentle stop right outside the large domed entrance. One of the smartly dressed doormen wearing a hat and long coat arrived as if by magic and opened the limo's doors to let the ladies out.

They could see Keith and Angela lingering just inside the imposing foyer but there was no sign yet of Mikey and Bernardo. As they all greeted each other, with lots of cheek kissing, another car pulled up with the boys inside. They fitted in well with the other sophisticated clientele, looking gorgeously dapper in black suits, white shirts and smart ties. Mikey greeted his parents with a kiss on each cheek, and Bernardo shook hands with them both. He introduced Bernardo to the ladies and as there were air kisses all around once more, Liv wondered whether all Portuguese men were so stylish. He looked very serious and Mikey looked downright petrified. She felt sorry for them both and hoped that the evening wasn't going to be too awkward for everyone.

She was glad of an excuse for them all to get dolled up this evening. They were wearing black, all having earlier expressed relief that they'd thought to bring a dressy dress on the holiday. Most women have that little black dress that can be brought out as an occasion dress.

Keith and Bernardo led the way through the foyer to the main casino area, where they wandered around observing the crowd for a few minutes and working out where they'd like to go first. It was starting to get busy. Their dining table was booked at nine and Liv was looking forward to seeing the show, before they took their chances at the variety of tables.

Liv linked arms with Mikey and patted his hand. 'Don't worry too much, darling, what will be will be. I'm a huge believer that everything happens for a reason. Just try to enjoy the evening. My parents, sadly, are no longer here for me to spend time with, so just appreciate the time you are getting to spend with yours while they're here. I don't mean to preach, but I'd give anything to spend the evening with my mum and dad.'

'You're right, Olivia. You know, you're quite wise. I do hope that this holiday has been everything you wanted it to be.'

'It's been way more than I wanted it to be already, Mikey, and thank you for making it all run so smoothly and for not saying anything about the cost of everything. The girls would never have agreed if I'd told them how much it really cost, and it really is so wonderful to be back with them. I've missed them more than they'll ever know.'

'Well, I hope you continue to have a wonderful time before you have to go home.'

'Hmmm. Home,' Liv muttered under her breath and a big cloud of sadness passed her eyes.

She looked up at Mikey. He was so handsome. He was going subtly grey at the temples, with strong cheekbones that most women would die for, and twinkling grey eyes that you got lost in. And such a kind, generous, considerate man. She really hoped that everything worked out for him. He did so much for others, and it was only fair that life was good to him too. She hoped that if anything did indeed come out of the woodwork this evening, that she could be there for him, because he'd never know what he'd done for her on this holiday. Facilitating her every wish had allowed her to have some clarity on what she wanted from her future. How she needed to change things dramatically when she got home, if she wanted to repair her broken family, before it was beyond mending.

When women came together it made them stronger, and she felt that spending a considerable length of time together, not snatching fifteen minutes for a phone call, had sparked things for all of them. This was just the start of the next part of all of their journeys. She felt that being with these dear friends for just this short time, had filled her full of something which had been missing from her life for a long time. Joy.

BERNARDO HELD THE door open for everyone to walk through into the bar restaurant and as Mikey walked past, he touched his hand. Mikey withdrew his hand immediately, acting as if an electric shock had gone through his body, because he saw that his father had clocked this action and he just didn't know how to react. He immediately wished he hadn't acted as he had when he saw the hurt on his lover's face. Mikey was so confused, but he did know, more than anything else in the whole world, that he didn't want to lose the love of his life and he knew that he had to do something about it. It had to be tonight.

The wonderful part about this casino was that there was a stage show while diners ate – and tonight's performance was spectacular. A troupe of super-talented acrobats performed the most incredible stunts, which had the audience up on their feet despite the waiters trying to serve food around them.

The meal was delicious, the Portugese rosé flowed, the company was fantastic and the laughter never stopped. They all got on like a house on fire, Bernardo and Keith laughing all the way through dinner. Mikey was so happy that they were getting on and hoped it might make things easier once he dropped his bombshell later.

As the crowds flowed out into the main casino area, Mikey took a deep breath and asked if he could have a word in private with his parents. He nodded at Bernardo, who escorted the women through to the bar area and ordered a round of drinks.

'Everything OK, son? This is all a bit serious.'

'I need you to sit down and listen to me. Please don't interrupt. I have something to say and I need to just come out and say it. This is something that's really hard for me and, to be totally honest,

I'm scared how you're going to react. OK?'

His parents both nodded at him, sitting down on the sofa opposite.

'Bernardo and I are partners.'

'That's wonderful news, darling. Has he given you shares in his company? He's a lovely man. What a nice thing to do.'

'No, Mum, not my business partner. My *partner* partner.' He let out a deep sigh and his shoulders slumped.

His mum looked at him with a puzzled expression on her face.

'But you told us Bernardo was married.'

'Yes I did. Because I was scared to tell you the truth. Because if you thought he was married you might not realise what he really means to me.'

His mother's face started to twitch. She looked at her husband, who was pulling the most expressive face and had started to cough uncontrollably. A waiter came over and placed a carafe of water and some crystal glasses on the coffee table between the two Chesterfield settees. Angela gave Keith a gentle thump on the back. When he got his breath back he pulled himself up straight and glanced at his wife. She nodded at him, before he looked his son once more in the eye.

'Michael, do you really think that you've got

this far through your life without us knowing that you're gay? What do you take us for?'

Mikey's mouth fell open. He couldn't find any words. All this time, he'd thought they didn't know. He'd thought they'd be disappointed with him, and that it would be a huge surprise to them, but here they were, saying that they already knew.

'You never said anything though, Dad. Mum?'

'And neither did you, son. If you weren't going to bring it up then neither was I. I know I'm your father, but it's not my business unless you choose to make it mine.'

'I couldn't find the words to tell you. I never came out to you. What will your friends say?'

Mikey's mother walked round to his side of the coffee table before she spoke. 'Michael, darling. We've known for years. I knew it before your father did and he didn't believe me at first. But over the years, it became obvious. But we didn't want to raise it because it might have been something you wanted to keep to yourself. You didn't need to come out for us to know. I carried you inside my body for nine months. You are part of me. I know you better than you think I do. More than that, you will always be my darling son, no matter whether you are gay, straight or trans. Who cares? I couldn't love you more and I could *never* love you less. I've seen the way you look at Bernardo. You love him. It's clear for everyone to see. And who cares what people say? You are our son and you always will be. We adore you and that will *never* change.'

A tear slid down Mikey's cheek and his breath caught in his throat. His emotions were all jumbled up. He'd kept this inside him for as long as he could remember. And all it had taken was a few words, put together to form one sentence, and it was done. He felt a huge weight had been lifted from his shoulders.

Keith stood and opened his arms and Mikey stepped into them. His dad squeezed him so hard. 'It's OK, son, it's really OK. I love you, you silly fool.'

Mikey's body shook with the emotion that had been simmering away inside him since the moment he met his parents at the airport.

His father let go and his mother enveloped him within her arms. 'I couldn't love you more than I do right now, my darling.'

He hugged his mum so tight. Tears streamed down both their cheeks when they parted.

'Right, go and wash your face and then we'd better get back to the others and put that gorgeous young man of yours out of his misery.'

He didn't quite know how his mother did it, but she always managed to make him feel as if he was thirteen years old. Normally he found that annoying, but right now it felt good. She winked at him and he grinned as he went off to the gents.

BERNARDO HAD UNDERSTANDABLY been on edge while Mikey was away. He had tried to include himself in the conversation with the ladies but kept looking up every time the door opened. He hoped that Mikey had the courage to go through with what he had promised to do tonight. If he didn't, Bernardo didn't know what the future held for the two of them. All he knew was that he didn't want to go on hiding their love for each other away from the world. He didn't want to be Mikey's dirty little secret. It made their relationship feel sordid and unimportant. And Mikey was the most important person in his life.

His family had taken Mikey into their fold with open arms and he loved how comfortable he felt amongst them. It would be wonderful if they could have something a little like that with Mikey's parents as well.

The door to the bar swung open and Keith, Mikey and Angela appeared, laughing as they came through. Bernardo looked at Mikey and Mikey nodded at him.

Bernardo stood and Keith walked over to him and held his hand out and shook it. Then he pulled Bernardo close to him in a bear hug. 'Welcome to the family, son.' Bernardo welled up with emotion and couldn't speak as Keith released him. Mikey grinned at him over his father's shoulder.

Angela walked forward. 'I have to say that my son obviously gets his fabulous taste in men from his mother.'

Bernardo laughed out loud and the atmosphere eased. Mikey walked over to his lover and hugged him.

'Steady on, boys. There's no need to flaunt it, you know.'

Angela thumped her husband on the arm for his joke, but there was so much love and laughter in the room at that particular time it didn't matter.

THE GIRLS ALL watched on, as if they were in the audience of a movie. Liv felt very emotional and wiped a tear from the corner of her eye. She knew how much it meant to Mikey to have the acceptance of his parents, and saw that he could not be happier as he looked across at her and beamed from ear to ear. She smiled back, delighted for him at how things had turned out. If he was one of her children, she would have reacted in exactly the same way as Angela and Keith clearly had. After meeting his parents last night, she'd thought that this was the exact reaction he'd get, but she was still pleased it had turned out that way.

Mikey walked across to Liv and kissed her cheek. 'Thank you, Olivia. You encouraged me and gave me the strength to feel brave enough to do this. You will never know just how close I came to losing him. I don't know what I would have done if that had happened. I've been so stupid.'

'But you didn't lose him, and you've done it now and all is OK. So it's time to move forward.'

As she said those words, she knew that it was time for her to be big and brave about her life too.

Chapter Twenty-Three

DEBS ANNOUNCED THAT spinning the roulette wheel was her favourite new pastime. She had already won over two hundred pounds and couldn't seem to stop herself wanting more. It was easy to see how see how people became addicted to gambling.

Samantha had given herself twenty euros to play with and once she'd lost that she was happy to just watch everyone else. She'd seen her husband gamble for huge stakes for years and saw what an impact it had on their lives. It scared her to death, and she'd vowed she'd never get taken in like he had.

Fiona appeared hypnotised by the flashing lights, robotic music and the metallic clonking of coins hitting the pay-out trays on the slot machines, which taunted you to put yet another coin in. But she had also set herself a limit and wouldn't go over it. Such restraint.

Liv loved watching her friends having a great

evening. She'd been to many casinos with George and watched him win thousands and lose thousands. It was something she couldn't get her head around, so had always steered clear of any of the gambling and had gone along for the experience more than anything. She loved to people-watch in a casino. She loved the glamour and the flamboyance of the clientele along with the plush surroundings and opulent art which adorned the walls. There were people playing for fun and people playing because they were desperate for money and only had this option to get it.

The croupiers and dealers looking super elegant in their designer suits, and the waiters and waitresses looked more like models, working the floor, taking drinks orders and being generously tipped, all added to the ambience and a fantastic night out, even though they all found it quite exhausting.

Her absolute favourite part of the evening, and a memory that would stay with her for ever, was when Mikey and Bernardo were standing next to each other leaning over a roulette table and Keith walked between the two of them, put his arms around their shoulders and gave them both a kiss on the cheek. Mikey and Bernardo linked hands behind Keith and the scene was perfection itself. Mikey had clearly been worrying for years over this delicate situation and Liv's heart swelled with pride for this kind-hearted man who had taken his son for who he was. She wished that there were more people in the world like him. If more people just loved and accepted everyone for who they were, the world would be a much kinder and better place.

At twelve forty-five, even though the casino was still a hive of activity, they decided to call it quits. Mikey called for the cars to take them all home and the girls dragged Debs away from the roulette wheel which had totally mesmerised her for most of the evening, or rather the handsome young croupier working on it who had been flirting outrageously with her.

Shouts of 'goodnight' and 'sleep well' could be heard down the street as Mikey's parents were dropped off at their gate and the ladies at theirs. Shattered, everyone headed for their bedrooms as soon as they got in. But after a while, when Liv realised that she couldn't sleep, she grabbed her phone from the drawer beside the bed, tiptoed downstairs to make herself a cup of tea, and sat out on the main terrace by the pool. It was so peaceful, she could hear the sea gently lapping at the shore at the bottom of the garden, and the stars shone like fairy lights in the clear sky above, casting twinkles on the water. She loved it here. She felt more at home here than she did actually *at* home. She knew she had some changes to make and with only two more days and one night ahead, she had better work out what they were going to be and how they were going to happen.

Even turning on her phone made her feel sick. She knew what to expect when she did. And as she'd feared, another barrage of text messages came through, not one of them asking if she was having a nice time, but every single one asking where something was, or how they did something, or where had she put something. She had hoped that a bit of time away from her family might do them all good, that every parent should have time away to put everything into perspective. Although where she thought that her time away would be about her missing them, she felt the exact opposite and was loving being away. That worried her. A lot.

The final voice message from George was a make-or-break message.

'Olivia, if you don't phone me back within twenty-four hours of leaving this message, there will be serious trouble.'

At that very minute, she didn't like her husband very much at all. Who did he think he was? And why couldn't he see why she'd done what she'd done? Yes, she'd gone away and switched her phone off so he couldn't get hold of her. But he wasn't worried about *her*. He was more worried about the things that were going on at home. And that was what upset her the most.

She couldn't think any more about it tonight. If she did, she might make a snap decision that she'd come to regret in time, so she pushed her worries to the back of her mind.

Fiona had been very quiet this week. Liv knew she felt guilty about putting her mum into respite while she came away, and that she kept going up to her room to do Facetime calls with Brenda to check on how her mum was getting on. She didn't say much about Marion and Liv wanted to encourage her to share how she was feeling. She would broach the subject over breakfast tomorrow and see if there was anything they could do to help her.

Debs was obviously loving spending time with Eduardo. She hadn't really said a lot, but the glint in her eye meant that she didn't need to. Liv was so happy for her. Goodness knows how that situation was going to pan out, but sometimes you just have to take a chance that's given to you. Debs was a grown woman and could make her own decisions and whatever she did in life, her friends would help and support her all the way.

And Samantha? Samantha seemed to have come out of her shell more since she'd admitted what had been going on with her son, and talked about the things she wanted to do with her life going forward. It was amazing how stuck in a rut you can sometimes become, but with just a little encouragement, she seemed to have really turned a corner in her life, planning lots of things for when she got home.

She loved these ladies so much. She felt sorry for people who didn't have friends like this. Friends who are not high maintenance in any way. Friends who you don't see all the time, but you know are totally there if you need them. She'd very much enjoyed this special time together. They'd made some lovely memories on the few days out; brunch at the marina, the day out at the market and playing golf, their evenings out and their evenings in too, chatting easily and amiably and helping each other to work out their issues.

Tomorrow, she was looking forward to a day lazing around the pool, topping up her tan and putting the world to rights with her wonderful friends.

Organising this holiday had been a mighty fine

idea, if she did say so herself. She knew they'd all get on well once the initial awkwardness of all being in the same house again after all these years had passed. It had been lovely to get to know each other all over again as grown women. Even though they'd keep in touch with phone calls once in a blue moon, she really wanted to make more of an effort once they got home and try harder to meet up more often – she hoped that they would all want to do the same. Life does get in the way, but friendship is so important and it's all about priorities.

When she thought about going home, the feeling of impending doom fell over her again. It was probably time for bed.

She grabbed a glass of water from the kitchen, and as she headed up the winding staircase, she heard low voices coming from Debs' room. She smiled to herself, thinking that one of the others must have slipped in to have a chat. Perhaps she should join them.

Just as she raised her hand, and was about to knock lightly, she heard a deep voice say, 'It's OK, they have gone' and a giggle from Debs. It obviously wasn't one of the others then. They didn't speak in a deep voice with a Portuguese accent. Liv smiled. Debs deserved some love and laughter in her life; she was really happy for her. She crept along the landing back to her own room and closed her door as quietly as she could.

WHEN DEBS HAD got to her room, she'd taken her off make-up and changed into a lovely long silk nightdress and slinky gown which she'd bought specially for the holiday because the lady in the department store told her that everyone deserved to look good in bedclothes. She went out onto the balcony to look at the view before bed, despite being shattered. Even in the dark, the view was stunning, the moonlit sky peppered with stars creating sparkles on the inky black sea, and the sound of the sea lapping at the shore at the bottom of the garden was so relaxing. She could stare at this view forever.

'Pssst!'

Debs had looked around but could see nothing and had thought she must be imagining things. She turned to walk inside and heard it louder this time.

'Pssst!'

She wandered over to the edge of the balcony and there on the side terrace was Eduardo.

She shook her head and placed her hand to her chest and in a loud whisper said, 'What on earth are you doing here?'

'I just wanted to say goodnight to you. I have been waiting for you to get back. I hope you had a wonderful evening. I just wanted to see you. I'm being quiet though. There is a light on downstairs and I think someone is on the terrace.'

Nothing like this had ever happened before to Debs. Romance like this was something she thought only happened in a Hallmark movie. Eduardo was a dream come true. And even if what they had was short-lived, she was determined she was going to bloody enjoy every single minute of it.

She giggled. 'You'd better come up!'

Eduardo grinned and disappeared round the side of the house and, just as she thought he'd gone for good, appeared carrying a ladder. She had to put her hand over her mouth to stop herself laughing out loud. He shimmied up the ladder as if this was a regular occurrence for him and climbed over the balustrade. He leaned down and kissed her fiercely. He stood back.

'You look…'

'Stupid? Fat? Old?'

'Beautiful.'

He took her hand and led her back inside. Debs tittered. They heard a noise out on the landing.

'Sshh! Someone is there!' she said, like a teen-ager who had been caught doing something they shouldn't have been by their parents.

They waited for a minute and heard nothing more.

'It's OK. They have gone,' Eduardo said.

He took her hand once more and led her to the bed, and showed her just how beautiful he thought she was.

Chapter Twenty-Four

'YOU OFF FOR a run again, Liv? Can I come with you?'

Debs was hovering outside Liv's door as she opened it.

'Keen, aren't you?' she laughed.

'I am. And I read somewhere that you have to make something that you really want to do a habit because if you give up easily, then it's harder to start it up again. I think it might have been Ronaldo who said that in an interview he did with Piers Morgan.'

'Oh, yes? And you do like a Portuguese man now, don't you?' Liv flicked her on the arm with her sports towel.

'I think you'll find that Ronaldo is from Madeira, actually.'

They both laughed as Samantha appeared from her doorway.

'Oh, I've missed your facts, Sam. I want facts from you all day today!' Liv laughed. 'You would so be my phone a friend option for that quiz show on the TV!'

'Facts all day, eh. Well, I'd love to be here for that that, but I'm off out with Eduardo again, aren't I?'

'I had forgotten that. You know, it's funny. I dreamt last night that he was in your room.' Liv stared at Debs who suddenly went bright red.

'Oh no, not another hot flush. This bloody menopause. You just don't know when it's going to hit, do you?' She started to fan at her face with her hands.

'Debs, there really is no need to hide anything from us. We're all delighted, and only a tiny bit jealous that you're getting it on with the gardener.' Samantha winked at her friend and Debs laughed. 'But I am glad you'll be back to come on the boat trip tonight. We would have really missed you. Where are you going on your day out? Come on, you can tell me about it while I fill our water bottles.' Samantha veered off at the bottom of the stairs towards the terrace, flinging herself on the nearest sunbed, feeling a little worse for wear after all of that rosé wine last night. She was determined to just sit and take in that perfect view for a while and think about nothing else.

Their run that day was a little more energetic.

Liv made Debs run a little further than the day before, and Debs found it slightly easier. She'd not drunk as much over the last couple of days and she'd been really careful with what she was eating too and already felt as if she'd lost a pound or two. Her leggings definitely felt a little looser on the waist this morning. She was determined that while she was on a roll she was going to continue to fight for her future self. Especially as she felt that she had something to fight for.

They had a light breakfast on their return from their run. Eduardo honked his horn at ten a.m. on the dot, and Samantha opened the door to him. He waited in the hallway, chatting about the weather, as Debs skipped down the stairs, dressed in a pair of cropped denim jeans, a pink strappy top and a pretty floral cardigan, stopping at the bottom to step into a pair of silver ballet pumps with jewels on the front. They completed her outfit beautifully. She was a little more prepared for a moped ride today.

Her skin was glowing and she couldn't stop smiling. She was high on life. Eduardo leaned across and kissed her right on the lips. Fiona and Samantha giggled like little girls and she screwed her eyes up and tutted in mock annoyance but blushed in front of her friends. They shooed her out of the door and watched and waved as they rode off.

'RIGHT, WHO'S FOR coffee?' Fiona asked.

'Me!' shouted Liv, who was fresh out of the shower. 'I'm going to do nothing but lie in the sun and top up my tan today.'

'You'd better make sure you have lotion on, lady! Stay safe and all that,' Samantha warned.

'Don't worry, I will, but I do need to top up my vitamin D levels. I love to feel the heat on my body.'

'Well, you'll find me under the umbrella with my book and my notepad,' Samantha said. 'I've got lots to think about and organise. I'm so excited about the future right now, and it's thanks to you guys. I can't thank you enough.'

'Seeing you planning all these things that you want to do is thanks enough, Sam, honestly. Life is for living. We're only here once and you realise that more the older you get, I think,' said Liv.

Fiona popped the tray of coffees onto the table and handed them round. Liv thought now was as good a time as any to try to tease some more information out of her.

'So, Fiona, how have you found it being away

from your mum for a few days? Has it been hard?'

'Oh, Liv. I don't know how I feel to be truthful. One minute it feels like a huge relief and the next I feel totally and utterly guilt-ridden. I've been talking to Brenda, such a nice lady.' Liv raised her eyebrows at Samantha who mirrored her actions. 'She's been telling me about the home and what sort of activities they do and advising that when Mum gets to the stage where I feel like I can't look after her any longer, then perhaps it would be better for her to be somewhere like that.'

'And how long do you think it might be till that time comes? Do you have any idea?'

'To be totally honest, I don't think it's that far away. I popped to the shops last week just to pick up a few bits. Mum seemed totally fine when I went out but when I got back I heard the smoke alarm going off. When I let myself in, she asked me who I was and what I was doing there. She was standing in the kitchen with a knife in her hand, and there was some toast in the toaster, which had burned and had set off the alarm. She said she didn't even remember putting the bread in the toaster but she did wonder why she had a knife in her hand. Thank God it was a blunt one. I think she's been getting progressively worse and I've been trying not to see it. But for her safety and mine it might be time to look at other options. I've put it off for this long but I think I need to make a plan. I can't really leave her alone in the house any more without someone sitting with her and I think I've pulled in all the favours I can from our neighbours for a while.'

'Oh, Fiona, that really is sad.' Liv reached across and stroked her arm.

'Coming away has been great, because it's made me realise that perhaps it is the best thing for both of us. As Brenda said, if Mum's in a home I can get back to being her daughter and the carers can look after her nursing needs. Brenda said that it's important at this stage of her illness to make new memories and talk about old ones, and to just enjoy each other's company.

'I must admit that sometimes I do have to walk away from Mum because I lose my patience at the simplest things. Like when she can't put her own knickers on and tries to put both legs down the same leg hole. Or there are times when she says that I've stolen something of hers and she doesn't know who I am. Brenda says that it won't be so frustrating when I'm only visiting and spending time with Mum. But I do have to get over the fact that I feel incredibly guilty that she may end her days in a home. It wasn't what I would have wanted in an ideal world. What if she never forgives me?'

'It must be hard, but Brenda sounds like she knows her stuff, so perhaps you should take note of what she's saying. And I suppose you also have to think of what the alternative is. You'd have to have practically full-time help at home, wouldn't you? How could you go and do any food shopping, or have any time to go to your own appointments and stuff, Fiona? You have to think about the practical side of things as well as the emotional,' said Liv.

She knew that if it was her in the same situation, she'd be in a complete quandary too. She felt incredibly sorry for her friend for this huge life-changing decision that she would have to make.

'I know it's not what you would have ideally wanted for your mum, but I don't suppose you ever thought that you'd both be in this particular situation either. Things change, Fiona and sometimes you have to change your ideals to make the best out of a less than perfect situation.'

'You are so right. And there are so many positives too. Families can still take residents out for the day, so I could bring her home every Sunday if she felt up to it. And they do organised trips where the families go along too and they have nursing and care support. It really does sound like the perfect solution for the future. I just don't know how far away it is at the moment. That's the bit that I've been trying to think about while I've been here. It's done me so much good to come away from the situation and have some thinking time. It's so full-on and all-consuming at home, it's hard to get your head round. Thank you so much, Liv, for organising this break and sorting everything. I think you're the only one of us who has an idea and just gets on with it and makes it happen. The rest of us just sit and ponder on how great it would be if it happened. You always were the most assertive one of us.'

Liv wondered how it was possible to be so assertive with things like this, but not in her own life.

'Ah, it's not been that difficult. I suppose I have plenty of time on my hands. And, to be honest, I just told Mikey what I wanted and he made most of the arrangements.'

Liv thought back to the initial phone call where she blurted out all her requirements to this person who had been recommended to her by one of the mums at school, a high-flying businesswoman who said that she couldn't live without him. Liv had written a huge list of what she wanted in her ideal scenario, expecting him to come back and say he could do some of the things on the list but not others, but he had just said that none of it would be a problem. She'd adored him from that moment on. It was amazing what money could get you.

'It's been quite a life-changing few days for all of us so far,' said Samantha. 'But what about you, Liv?' she nervously asked.

'Oh God! Is it my turn now?' she laughed bitterly. 'I suppose I've dodged it for long enough, haven't I?' She inhaled and then exhaled slowly. 'Well, I have come to the conclusion that I'm just an ungrateful cow. I have everything that I could ever want, and lots of things that others would love to have, but I'm not happy. What does that say about me?' She wiped away a tear that was rolling down her cheek.

'I don't have to work, I have two beautiful children, a gorgeous husband who gives me anything I ask for, money if I want it, a fabulous house that most people would give their right arm for, and yet the only one in that house that loves me for me is the dog. My darling Hector. All I am to everyone else is a taxi driver, maid, secretary, cook… shall I go on? Now tell me that I'm not a selfish bitch.' She sniffed away another tear.

'I would never think that of you as that.' Samantha came and sat on the end of Liv's sunbed and handed her a tissue. 'What would you say to us in this situation, Liv? I know exactly what you'd say. Sometimes you have to evaluate your life and think about changes, sometimes big and sometimes small, that you can make, to make things better. You know this. It's what you've been helping us with while we've been here. And it's something you're brilliant at. Now you just need to do it for yourself. Let us help you, Liv, like you've helped us. Sometimes others can see things that you can't see but are just within your reach.'

Liv nodded at her friend, knowing she was right.

'Now I'm going to go upstairs and fetch a new notepad and a pen and we're going to sit here and brainstorm some things which you could change or add into your life which would make you happy,' said Samantha. 'I read a feature in the magazine you get on the plane about someone famous – I can't remember who it was now, and it doesn't matter anyway – who said that you need to do things in life which bring you joy. So we're going to help you to put the joy back into your life, the same way you've helped us.'

How did people cope without wonderful friends in their life? Liv thanked God that she was one of the lucky ones who was surrounded by them.

Chapter Twenty-Five

EDUARDO STEADILY DROVE the moped on the twenty-minute journey from Vilamoura into Albufeira so that Debs could take in as much of the scenery as possible. As they entered the town, he found a parking space outside a hotel and helped Debs to dismount. It wasn't her most elegant moment ever, and they laughed as she wobbled and caught her foot on the seat and nearly toppled the bike, Eduardo and herself to the ground. Being with Eduardo made her realise that she hadn't laughed for such a long time. And it felt good to laugh. She felt as if she'd had a permanent grin on her face since the moment she'd stepped off the plane at Faro airport.

He took her hand and she righted herself and he leaned across and kissed her passionately on the lips. She loved the way he took every moment he could to do that and he made her feel as if she was worth a million dollars. She would miss him so much when she got home, even though she hadn't known him for long. This short time had been so very special to her. It had changed her life and she would *never* forget it. Sadness started to engulf her, but she pushed it away. She was determined to make the most of every moment and have a fabulous day.

Wandering around the narrow, cobbled streets in Albufeira, which were packed with tourist shops on either side, and market stalls selling leather goods, jewellery and clothing, she didn't know where to look first. They walked up a slight hill – amongst the busy families clearly on holiday, and snapping up cheap and tacky souvenirs – and through an archway to see the sea glistening in front of them, the waves twinkling prettily in the sunlight. Restaurants, bars and benches overlooked the sea.

A tall, rugged-looking man approached them and held his arms out to Eduardo. They hugged and he heartily clapped him on the back and a torrent of Portuguese words flowed from both of them. They were clearly good friends.

'And this is my very good friend, Debs. Debs, this is an old family friend, Tito.'

Tito moved forward and shook her hand. 'Good to meet a friend of this wonderful man. Come this way, my friends. I will show you to your table.'

They walked across a short wooden boardwalk, laid on top of the golden sand, towards a stunning building with very old brick walls and turquoise window frames. Palm trees in pots surrounded the entrance and rattan furniture was placed under parasols to create some shade from the already powerful rays of the mid-morning sun. They settled at a table overlooking the sea and the potent smell of baking hit Debs' nose and she filled her lungs with the delicious smell.

Tito appeared with a large cafetière and two stoneware mugs coated in a beautiful azure blue glaze which matched the exact colour of the sea just in front of them, along with a plate full of warm, freshly baked pastries.

'Tito is the most amazing baker,' said Eduardo. 'I've missed your pastries. And you too, of course.' He grinned at his friend.

'Then you should visit me more, minha amiga. You are too busy working all the time. You have to have some fun in your life too. Although maybe you are now.' He winked at Debs.

She, in turn, looked at Eduardo who was watching her adoringly. She appreciated that they had spoken in English so that she could understand them, although as Tito turned to walk away, they reverted to their native tongue for a brief exchange.

'I love the sea,' said Debs. 'I could sit and just stare at it for hours. It makes me feel at peace. I feel like it fills me up, if that doesn't sound too silly. I feel like it fills my soul.' A flush crept across her cheeks and she turned away from him and breathed in the salty air. A sailboat caught her eye, far out at sea. Eduardo smiled at her.

'Thank you for bringing me here. I love Portugal. How have I never been here before? This view is incredible. And these pastries look divine.'

Debs was torn between wanting to try Tito's baked goods and trying her hardest to resist them, but the smell was so overwhelming that she couldn't help but take one. She vowed to run a little bit further tomorrow to work it off. She closed her eyes and sighed as the soft, buttery pastry melted on her tongue and then the sweet jam hit her taste buds.

'Mmmm! Just delicious!'

'He is the best pastry chef I know. I wish you had time to try everything on the menu. Oh Debs. There is so much of my beautiful country that I want to show you. I hope that one day soon, you might consider coming back and letting me show you more.' He brought her hand to his lips and kissed it. 'I wish you didn't have to go home when we are just getting to know each other.' He leaned towards her and sighed. 'Tell me more about your life in England. I want to know everything about you.'

'There is not much to tell you, to be honest. I lead a very dull life at home. I go to work, I come home. I watch TV. I have a few friends at work and we go out once a fortnight, to quiz night at our local pub, or to bingo, but to be honest that's it. All very boring.'

As she said this, she realised that she didn't have much of a life at all and that was perhaps why she'd jumped at the chance to come away when Liv had rung her to suggest it. She drifted off in her head and imagined how it would be to live somewhere like this town they were visiting. Somewhere you could just come and drink coffee by the sea and watch the world go by. It would feel so very different. Nothing like going to the local coffee shop by yourself really dreading the fact that you might bump into your ex and his new girlfriend, who used to be your friend.

Eduardo was very lucky to live somewhere with all this on his doorstep. Perhaps she *should* think about moving to the coast when she got home. She had always loved the sea, and now that she and Dave had gone their separate ways, there was no real reason to be landlocked in the Midlands. She felt a little frisson of excitement as she thought about this possibility of a different future. Perhaps she could take some time off work and visit a few places on the coast to see what might be possible. She'd chat to the girls about it tonight. She knew they'd tell her the truth. They'd either encourage her, or tell her that it was an unrealistic dream.

As a child she used to spend lots of time at the coast at her Aunty Wynne's house. She was Debs' nan's sister and she had many cherished memories of her nan taking her down to her sister's in Mudeford in Dorset for the school holidays and them going crabbing on the quay. She'd always said she wanted to live in that part of the world when she was older. How could she have forgotten this? How was it that as you grew up and real life took over and you became part of a couple, your dreams sometimes got quashed and their dreams, or lack of them in Dave's case, became the focus of your life?

She realised that by the end of her marriage, she and Dave spent most nights sitting on the sofa in their tracksuits, because they were comfy and because they both felt they didn't need to make an effort with each other. They had nothing in common any more and didn't have any dreams about the future. It was all about existing in the here and now, and living for a Chinese takeaway and *Strictly Come Dancing* on a Saturday night. And that wasn't what she had wanted from her life.

For the first time since she and Dave split up, Debs realised why he had gone off with Perfect Penny. She was young and vibrant, and excited about life. All the things that Debs hadn't been any more.

But all the things that she had been thinking about right then, sitting by the sea with Eduardo, made her feel in love with life again and feel possibilities for her own future, whether she was alone or not. Perhaps it was time she took control of her own destiny and made her own dreams come true.

EDUARDO PULLED HER to her feet. 'Come! We have lots to see today before I deliver you back to your friends for your boat trip.'

She laughed, feeling lighter in her heart than she had felt for years.

A short moped ride took them to Guia, where they parked up in a dusty car park, and Eduardo produced two small towels from the seemingly bottomless panier on the back of the moped. The walked on the short boardwalk to the beach and laid the towels out on the sand. They kicked off their shoes and paddled carefree in the sea, holding hands and giggling like toddlers, jumping the waves as the cold water of the Atlantic Ocean splashed their feet. Grabbing an ice cream from one of the beach vendors, they sat on the rocks, licking at their ice creams, watching the waves lap at the shore, watching the world go by, and as Eduardo draped his arm around Debs' shoulders she felt safe, loved and happy.

Being with him felt so different to how she'd felt with Dave in their more platonic relationship. She reminded herself to stop comparing the two men and take this exactly for what it was, a brief holiday fling, which had introduced her once more to the joys in life. But oh boy, she was going to miss Eduardo when she got back to her dreary life back home. She snapped a selfie of them sitting there, which she knew she would print out and put on her mantelpiece to remind her of the person she was while she was with this lovely man, and to remember that this, whatever this was, had really happened.

TIME SEEMED TO be flying by, and Debs hated that

they were watching the clock to make sure she got back to the villa in time to go out, even though she was looking forward to spending the evening with the girls on the boat trip. Their precious time together was flying by and she was determined to make every minute count with her friends, as well as Eduardo.

Their final journey, in the mid afternoon, took them to the small town of Quarteira, where her friends had so enjoyed the markets. Eduardo pulled up in a narrow side street and when they dismounted from the moped, put a key in the lock of a door in a large, arched doorway, which looked like it was in desperate need of a lick of paint. Eduardo held onto her hand tightly as they walked through a cool, dimly lit, tiled hallway, and up a flight of stairs. Debs was really not expecting what she saw when they reached the gallery landing at the top of the stairs, and she gasped as she took it all in. A whitewashed room, with white leather settees, adorned with peacock-blue, hot-pink and lime-green cushions, formed the most delightful seating area. But it was the view that took her breath away. Through French doors, the sunlight twinkled away on the turquoise sea, which looked so close she felt that she could reach out and touch it.

'Oh my!' she whispered.

'Welcome to my home.'

'Oh, Eduardo. It's stunning, just stunning.' She couldn't tear her eyes away from the vista before her.

Eduardo opened the French doors and led Debs by the hand onto a huge roof terrace which was like another outside room. Another seating area, with rattan furniture faced out towards the sea. A canopy hung from the doorframe, offering shade if needed. A pergola covered a dining area on the far side of the terrace, and a lone hammock was situated in the other corner. 'It's just beautiful. What an amazing home you have.'

'Thank you. Let me show you around.'

He led her into a bright modern kitchen area, impeccably clean, just off to the right of the lounge, and a twin-bedded guest room to the left. A large modern bathroom with the hugest shower she'd ever seen sat to the left of that. The final door led to Eduardo's bedroom, which also had access to the vast terrace.

'Oh, how would you ever tire of that view? I love it. It feels so peaceful and full of joy. You are so lucky to live here, Eduardo.'

They walked out onto the terrace once more and he pointed out to the right the promenade which led all the way into Vilamoura – should a leisurely walk take someone's fancy. And to the left, there was a long stretch of sandy beach. There was a beach bar in the distance, which Eduardo explained was owned by a very good friend. Debs sighed. It was perfect.

He led her back into the bedroom and sat down on the bed, patting the space beside him. She joined him and their limbs intertwined as they fell back onto the mattress and desire took over.

After slow and sensual love-making, Eduardo pulled Debs close.

'Stay!'

Debs drew back and stared at him. Did he really just say that? She didn't know whether he was serious. He looked it, but she realised once more that she didn't know him at all well, and had no idea whether he was jesting with her.

She smiled. 'Now, isn't that a nice thought?'

'Doesn't have to be just a thought, Debs. Seriously, what do you have to go back to, a job you don't like? You said yourself that your life was dull. We are at an age in life where we have to take chances. Seize the moment. Maybe things won't work out, but what if they did? And if we don't try, we'll never know. These last few days have been wonderful. You make me smile. You make my heart sing. Just think, you could wake up to this beautiful view every day.' He ran his hands over his chest and then opened his arms out to the sea.

She laughed. 'You or that?'

'Both. Please, Debs. Just think about it. I have never felt like this about anyone. I just want to be with you.' He pulled the throw from the bottom of the bed and covered them both, drawing her into his arms. She lay with her head against his chest listening to his heart beating. She was totally discombobulated.

She couldn't stop hearing that one word. That very short but very powerful word, which could change her whole life. Stay.

EDUARDO LOOKED AT his watch. 'Carinho, I am sorry, but I think we have to make moves. Your friends will be waiting.' Debs retrieved her clothes, which in the heat of passion had been abandoned and scattered across the floor. They were both quiet, their thoughts taking over. She stood, leaning on the doorframe which led out to the terrace, breathing in the sea air and committing this magnificent view to memory, and wondered if she would ever see it again.

Eduardo touched her lightly on the arm, startling her from her bubble. Sadly, she pulled herself away from this beautiful sight only for Eduardo to draw her towards him and kiss her firmly on the lips. 'This could all be yours. You just have to say yes. Easy, yes?' He winked at her. 'Come on.'

She had the choice of two very small words. One with two letters and one with three. Why were all these life-changing words so small and unassuming? But at the same time, so huge and significant.

Arriving back at the villa, they dismounted and he took her in his arms. 'Just think about it, my love. Please. Chances like this don't come along often in a lifetime and sometimes we just have to grab them. Text me when you get back later and if you want me to, I'll come over to see you.'

She clung onto him for dear life, and then they parted and she walked towards the villa. She looked over her shoulder and raised a hand, before the man who had stolen her heart drove away from her.

Liv was sitting in the lounge as she walked in. 'We have to leave in about half an hour, darling. That OK for you?' Debs nodded not trusting herself to speak and Liv must have noticed that her eyes were full of tears. 'Everything OK, Debs?'

'Yep, just need to go and get ready. Back as quick as I can.'

OMG! What a quandary she had now. What a decision to make. Should she share it with the others or did she need to get her head around it first? If she went home, she could regret it for the rest of her life, but if she stayed and they tired of each other, it might not work out. She had some serious thinking to do. She threw off her clothes and jumped into the shower, wanting to stay there forever and not have to make the most important decision she'd ever had to make in her life.

Chapter Twenty-Six

LIV NOTICED THAT despite the fact that Debs' eyes were sparkling, and she was glowing, she was unusually quiet on the journey into Vilamoura. She must try to grab her alone later and ask if everything was OK. She hoped that nothing bad had happened on her day out with Eduardo today. She hoped he hadn't upset her in any way. Perhaps she was just sad because they were leaving soon. God, the thought of that made her heart race again. She still hadn't come to a firm decision about her own life and how things were going to change when she got home, and she didn't have long to sort it out.

The driver pulled up at a security gate, opposite the Tivoli Marina Hotel, and the friends alighted from the car. It was just after five p.m. and they could still feel the heat of the sun on their shoulders. The marina was already a bustling hive of activity, tourists checking out the yachts of the rich and famous, and people starting their evenings early, before the dining scene began to heave.

'Good evening, ladies, my name is Martin and my brother Jason and I will be your crew on the yacht this evening. Would you like to come this way?'

Fiona raised her eyebrows at Samantha, both of them unable to believe that they had such a handsome skipper.

Martin led them down the walkway towards a large white yacht.

'It's called a passarelle, you know. Often mistakenly called the gangplank,' Samantha muttered.

'Been on the internet again have you, Sam?' Fiona asked, and the ladies all laughed good-naturedly.

'You'll be glad I have when you want to know everything later,' she quipped back.

'Welcome to *Lady Marmalade*,' said Martin. He took each of their hands as he helped them onto the lower deck. He pointed up to the helm. 'And up there is my trusty sidekick Jason, who is just carrying out the final safety checks.' Jason gave them a wave and a comic salute from the top of the yacht. 'Take a seat, ladies, and make yourselves nice and comfortable. Let me get you some drinks.'

'OMG! This is gorgeous!' Debs seemed to be

coming out of herself now they'd got onto the boat and was back to being enthusiastic about their surroundings. 'I've *never* done anything like this before. In fact, I don't think I've ever been on a boat before, unless you count the ferry to the Isle of Wight.'

The pop of a champagne cork made them look round as Martin appeared with a bottle of fizz and poured them all a glass.

'An occasion like this deserves a toast, don't you think? Which of you lovely ladies is going to say a few words?'

Liv spoke up. 'May I?' They all nodded. 'I'd like to thank you all for agreeing to come away this week. To spend quality time with you all, after all these years, has been the absolute best tonic and I have loved every minute. Thank you all so much for your company. I love you all dearly. Cheers, ladies. To us and our futures.'

They clinked glasses and called their favourite Corfu phrase 'Yamas' loudly and sipped at their drinks. They all seemed excited about what the future held for them when they got home, yet Liv felt differently as she knew that there could be trouble ahead one way or another.

Martin placed a bowl of olives on a table, with some bread sticks and canapés.

'A little snack to start you on your way. Dinner will be served around seven p.m. We'll be serving barbecued sea bass, pan-fried Mediterranean vegetables and sauté potatoes with sea-salt and rosemary. I do hope that's OK for everyone.' There were nods all round. They all thought it sounded divine.

'So, shortly we'll set sail. We'll go out into the ocean and towards the caves, and then we'll head out to see if we can find you any dolphins before we catch the magnificent sunset on our way back into the marina. Do feel free to wander around the yacht. If you'd like to go up front, I do insist that you wear a life jacket. He gave a short demonstration as to how to wear the life jackets and showed them where they were kept. And if you get chilly at all, there are some blankets just inside. Oh and I'm sure you'll want to know that the loo is down the steps, to the lower decking and on the left. And if any of you would like to try your hand at driving this beauty, just let us know. Any questions?' He was met with silence and shaking heads all round. 'Great. So we're good to go. All set, ladies?'

They all nodded excitedly, like eager toddlers waiting for a pantomime to start.

Martin flashed his white teeth in a Hollywood film-star smile and turned to give Jason the thumbs-up sign, and they heard the engine thrum deeper as the yacht started to gently move away from the mooring. The ladies grinned at each other as they took in the sights and sounds of the marina from a different angle. As the marina started to get further and further away, the yacht picked up speed and Jason grinned as he booted the engine and the boat dipped on one side as they started their journey towards the open sea, leaving a trail of white bubbles and froth behind them.

WHEN THE INITIAL excitement settled, the four friends gazed out to sea, staggered that the coastline disappeared so quickly from sight. People on beaches now were dots in the distance.

'Right, I'm going up front! Who's coming with me?' said Samantha.

She steadily made her way to the bow, holding on tightly to the rails, stopping to pick up a life jacket on the way.

'Come on, let's all go. You only live once and if we fall in, I'm sure Martin and Jason will do a *Baywatch*-style rescue.' Liv started to follow Samantha.

'Worth falling in, just for that picture alone,' Debs roared.

'This is so exhilarating! Come on, girls. Selfie time! I'm like the lady on the "Rio" video by Duran Duran! But that gorgeous cow never had to wear a bright-yellow bloody life jacket!' Samantha laughed and plonked herself at the front of the boat. 'It's called the bow, you know.'

'Sam, do shut up!'

Liv threw a pillow she'd brought from the back of the boat at Samantha, and she threw her head back and let the wind rush through her hair, trying to get them all in the picture at the same time as balancing. It wasn't easy. The others didn't have the heart to tell her she looked like a wild woman right now; she was clearly having the time of her life. Liv had had the foresight to scrape her hair back into a neat ponytail, and Debs, in her rush to get ready, had put hers up with a clip. Fiona had short cropped hair, anyway, and loved that it hardly took any caring for, even though her mum had once asked the postman who the man was in her house that day and he'd had to explain that it was her own daughter. She smiled at the memory. She had to or else she'd cry.

After half an hour or so, they were moving in closer to the coast, heading through crystal-clear turquoise water to the rugged headland where an archway through the rocks led to caves beyond.

They didn't stay long, as the daylight was starting to dwindle, but the stunning sight of the inside of the caves was another thing that Fiona was committing to memory. She'd found herself doing this a lot lately; closing her eyes and picturing what she could see, trying to almost put a photograph in her memory bank. When there was so much that her mum couldn't remember, she wanted to make sure she was capturing as many of her memories as she could while she had the chance. She would make sure that when she got back to the villa and before she went to sleep, she wrote everything down. Every sight, every sound, every smell and every taste.

After the boat turned and the caves were left behind, they headed away from the rocky headland outwards the open sea. The sun was starting to descend. The evening sky was turning into a blend of rich gold, deep orange and red, the sun a glowing fireball in the distance. A truly spectacular sight.

'Look! To the right! Dolphins!' Martin yelled.

Three dolphins playfully darted through the wake of the boat, taking it in turns to dance and jump through the air, then glide gracefully back into the water. Samantha reached for her phone and began to snap away as everyone gazed in awe at this spectacular sight, amazed by these magnificent creatures in their natural habitat. As the boat pulled closer towards the coastline again, the majestic dolphins swam away, back out where the sea was deeper.

Martin appeared back on deck. 'I'm so happy you got to see them. They don't always join us, so we've been very lucky this evening.' He placed a plate of bread and tuna paste on the table, along with some knives. 'I hope you are all hungry as I'm nearly ready to serve. Now, who's for wine?'

The boat's engine stopped thrumming and Jason said that he'd dropped the anchor so that he and Martin were free to join the ladies for dinner. They were great company, entertaining them with tales of some of the nightmare and hilarious passengers that they'd taken on the boat over the years.

When the ladies were absolutely stuffed from the delicious meal they'd eaten every last morsel of, Martin and Jason cleared away and disappeared below deck once more. Phones were taken out of handbags, the glorious breath-taking and spectacular sky demanding that more photos were taken. Martin took a photo of the four of them with the sunset in the background, and they all knew in their hearts that it would be this photograph that would be the one that they put on their mantelpieces to remind them of a wonderful trip and an awesomely inspiring holiday.

MARTIN CAME AROUND with a coffee pot and they all huddled around the mugs, noticing the start of a chill in the air. Two minutes later, Jason appeared with a selection of blankets and fleecy throws for the guests to wrap around their shoulders. The sky was turning deeper red and magenta hues replaced the gold-and-orange ones from earlier, giving even more depth to the sunset as the evening went on. Jason went back up to the helm and shouted for Martin to join him. There were muted whispers and furtive glances towards the women. Martin came back down, scratching at his stubble, and clapped his hands together, and in a voice which seemed a little more forced than before, offered more drinks.

Liv looked at her watch. She thought they would have been on their way back by now, that they were due into the marina from around nine thirty to ten p.m. It was nearly nine thirty now and they didn't seem to be even thinking about getting back. She couldn't put her finger on it, but her intuition was telling her that something wasn't right. She caught Martin's eye and he smiled at her, then quickly looked away chewing the inside of his cheek before he disappeared down the stairs.

She stood and said she was just popping to the loo, and bumped into Martin who was on his way back up, just as she came out of the small cubicle.

'Everything OK, Martin? What time are we heading back?'

'Ah, well, I wasn't going to say anything, but as you are on your own, I'll tell you and perhaps we can work out what to do. I'm so sorry, Mrs Pemberton, but we seem to have a slight problem with the engine right now, which Jason has been trying to work on. But it's getting later and I think we should probably call it in to the coastguard. I think we need some help. Hopefully they'll send out a rescue boat for us. I just didn't want everyone to panic. Do you want me to tell the others, or would you like to?'

Liv's heart sank. Blooming great. It had been such a perfect night up till now.

'I suppose I will. How long do they normally take to come out?'

'Normally within a couple of hours.'

'*A couple of hours?*'

'Please keep your voice down, Mrs Pemberton. I don't want anyone to be scared.'

'Oh for God's sake! This is a nightmare. What a way to spoil a night.'

'If it's any consolation, this has *never* happened to us before.'

'No, it's not any consolation, to be honest. I'd rather it hadn't happened at all. But it has. I'll go and tell the others.'

Liv went back out to the top deck, followed closely behind by Martin.

'Girls, I have something to tell you, and I don't want you to panic.'

Martin put his head in his hands. If there was one phrase to make people scared when you don't want them to be, that was the one.

'What's happened, Liv?' Fiona looked petrified.

'What it is, Liv? Just spit it out.' Samantha raised her voice.

'There's a problem with the engine and we're not going anywhere without any help. Martin has—'

'What the hell? Are you saying we're stranded out at sea?' Debs asked. 'What time are we likely to get back? I'm meeting Eduardo when we get home. I'll have to let him know that I'm going to be late.' Debs picked up her phone but, to her dismay, noticed the words 'NO SIGNAL' on her display. 'Oh, great! So not only are we stuck in the middle of a fucking great ocean, we've got no phone signal either.'

Martin headed over to the group. 'Ladies, I am so sorry. I can assure you this has never happened before. We carry out full safety checks before every journey and today was no exception. But the engine appears to have developed a problem and we can't get it started. Jason has called the coastguard and they'll send someone out to us as soon as possible. I can assure you that you are all quite safe, but I cannot apologise enough.'

Liv shivered. The nip in the air they'd felt earlier, and the panic that had set in, despite Martin's protests to not be scared, was definitely starting to take a toll on them all. Martin brought out extra blankets to them and asked them if they'd rather be below deck, but they said that they would prefer to be above water level and wrapped themselves up. Samantha had gripped Fiona's hand and Debs had wrapped her arms around herself and started to tap her foot impatiently.

Oh God. They had to stay calm. Liv hoped that the coastguard was going to be with them soon. This trip had turned into a disaster.

Chapter Twenty-Seven

'OMG! WHAT IF no one finds us and we die here out at sea?' Debs stood up theatrically and waved her arms around.

'Don't be ridiculous, Debs. We're just stranded for an hour or so. Stop being so melodramatic. You always have to dramatise every situation.'

'I do not, Samantha. There's no need to be nasty.'

'Well, stop being an attention-seeking drama queen then!' This time it was Fiona who spoke up. 'We're all scared. It would be nice if we helped each other stay calm instead of winding each other up.'

Debs huffed and flopped back down, wrapping herself back up in a blanket.

'Look, we all need to stay calm. We just have to wait till someone comes and helps us. It shouldn't be too long.' Liv was always the voice of reason, had been all her life with these ladies. She giggled.

'This is hardly a time to laugh, Olivia.' She knew she was in trouble when Debs called her by her full name.

'I'm just finding it funny that we've all reverted to our twenty-one-year-old selves. Debs the drama queen, Liv the sensible one, always trying to calm down any situation, and Fiona and Samantha huddled together, pretending that whatever is happening, actually isn't.'

Debs' mouth started to turn up at the corners until she broke out into a grin. 'I thought I'd grown out of that. It's you lot. You make me do it.'

'Oh and now you blame everyone else as usual.' Fiona laughed.

'Nothing is ever your fault is it, Debs?' Samantha joined in.

'I bloody love you lot. Do you know that?'

'I need to tell you all something.' Samantha pursed her lips together. 'I haven't told a soul this but I had a bit of a scare recently when I found a lump in my breast. Luckily, it was just a "gristly lump of fat", the doctor said. Gross, isn't it? But until I had the results, I didn't know if it was something more sinister and I don't mind telling you that I was bloody scared.'

Fiona reached across and squeezed her hand.

Samantha smiled sadly, remembering how numb she'd felt at the time.

'I'm one of the lucky ones, though. When I came out from seeing the consultant after he'd told me that it needed removing but wasn't cancer, seeing people who were clearly having treatment and looked so ill made me realise that life is so precious and I'm fed up of wasting time. I've wasted years being stuck. When Robert died, I bottled up my anger with him just to get Peter and I through it, and now it's time to deal with it once and for all and for things to change.

'Being with you all, just for a few days, has made me realise that I love being with people and that I'm lonely. But I'm determined now that I need to do something about it. So all those suggestions you made for me, so I can make some changes to my life, really couldn't have come at a better time. I really am most grateful.'

'Good for you. I'm so proud of you,' said Liv. 'I'm sorry it took a cancer scare to make you feel this way, but I always worried about you throwing yourself into making sure Peter was OK after his dad died, and I honestly think you never properly grieved yourself.'

'I think you are absolutely right, Liv. When Peter left to go to university last September, it was the first time I actually sat and thought about Robert and how I felt. I actually had some counselling and it felt good to tell someone that I didn't know how angry I was with him. I knew that they wouldn't judge me and I could say anything and it would go no further. It really helped me to come to terms with everything and eventually forgive myself for feeling the way I did but more than that, forgive Robert. Forgiveness is a powerful tool. Forgiving someone isn't about the fact that they deserve forgiveness but about the fact that you deserve peace in your life and not to be dragged down.' There were nods all round. That made a lot of sense.

'He let us all down so badly before he died and I've kept people at a distance, but I've never felt so lonely in my life. Then there's Peter. I send him texts and he doesn't respond. I wait for half term so he can come home, and he decides to stay with friends instead. I've sat and cried and cried until I felt that I had no tears left. Peter's fine, he's getting on with his life and it's time that I got on with mine. Being his mum was all I wanted to do. My favourite thing in the whole world, but now I'm left with nothing. And despite everything that Robert did, I did love him very much and he wouldn't want me to be sad. I bet if he was here instead of me, he'd be living it up. He certainly did while he was alive, not caring whether he could afford it or not. I *can* afford it, so that's what I'm going to do. I just might need your help, girls.'

'You've got all the help you need, honey. We're all here for each other. Always have been. Always will be.' Liv reached across and patted her arm again.

'I'm scared that I'm going to get dementia too!' They all turned to look at Fiona as she blurted out the words she'd been holding inside for so very long. 'I can look after Mum, but if I get it, who is going to look after me? Will I end up in a home with people I don't know wiping my backside and cutting up my dinner because I've forgotten how to do it? Oh, and I think I'm a lesbian too. I think I'm in love with Brenda.'

'Jeez, Fiona,' Liv giggled. 'Have you only just realised that? We've all known that part of it for years!'

A round of giggles swept across the table.

'Seriously? Have you really? And you don't mind?' she asked.

'Why would we mind?' Liv asked.

'I did wonder if you were going to come on to me once,' Debs confessed.

'Don't flatter yourself, Debs. I might be a lesbian, but it doesn't mean that I'm up for any old slapper, you know.'

Debs roared with laughter. Fiona's sense of humour had been seriously compressed on this holiday. In the past she'd always been the one who made them smile in the worst of any situation and Debs was glad that the old Fiona seemed to be back.

'Is dementia hereditary?' Samantha asked.

'The majority of dementia is not inherited, but when people develop it at an earlier age, there is a larger possibility that it's the type that can be passed through the generations, even though it's quite rare. But I've become obsessed with it recently. That's why I'm so obsessed with being healthy, as it can help to prevent vascular dementia. It's such an unfair disease. I hate seeing Mum the way she is. It's so sad. You can send me on a one-way flight to Switzerland if I ever have to go through what she's going through. It's such a cruel disease.'

'Eduardo has asked me to stay here in Portugal with him!' Debs burst out her revelation.

'Jeez, Debs. Change the subject, why don't you? That's a turn-up for the books. You've only just met him. What are you going to do?' asked Liv.

'I really don't know. I went to his house today. It's stunning. It overlooks the sea. My house overlooks a brick wall that all the kids play football up against and I know I probably haven't told you this before, but I really don't love my job that much. It certainly doesn't make me want to jump out of bed every morning. Coming here and meeting Eduardo has made me think that I'm so lost in life and reminded me that I've always wanted to live by the sea. But do I do it here or do I move to the coast at home? I really don't know. But as the holiday is coming to an end and we're supposed to be flying home soon, I suppose I need some help from you guys to make a decision. All I know is that I have never felt like this about anyone in my life, and I'm scared that I might *never* feel like this again.'

'But you've only just met him, Debs,' Liv reminded her.

'You think I don't already know that? I hardly know him and this is the biggest, scariest decision that I'll ever have to make. Do I want to take the risk of being hurt again? Dave leaving me, nearly broke me. But, I thought at first that I couldn't live without him, but then I realised that I could. Do I want to go through it all again? But the thing that worries me the most is that I'll never be able to give him children.'

'You're fifty years old, Debs, I think he's probably worked that out for himself. And you never wanted children anyway. You've always said that,' said Liv.

'Yes, I did say that. But the one thing that I've *never* shared with anyone is that I *couldn't* have children.' She took a deep breath and carried on, her voice wobbling. 'I had an abortion when I was younger, when I first met Dave, and it went horribly wrong.' Debs began to sob. 'I haven't told you this yet but just before I came out tonight, Dave sent me a text to tell me that bloody Penny is pregnant, so she's giving Dave something I could never give him and that breaks my heart. So it's alright for you, Mrs Perfect, with your perfect house and your perfect family and your perfect life. We're not all as lucky as you, you know.'

Liv didn't even hesitate before firing back at her.

'You know what, Debs? You know *nothing* about me and my life. So get your facts straight before you go shooting your mouth off. For your information, and while we're all getting our confessions out on the table, I seriously don't want to go home and am thinking about telling George and the boys that I'm not going back. I *cannot* go back to a life where I'm not happy. Life is for living and I'm just skivvying around after them. I'm just not going back to *that* life. Do I leave them? Do I find myself somewhere else to live? Or do I stay here too? Can I come and live with Eduardo? Does he have a spare room?' Liv laughed at the horrified expression on Debs' face. 'That last bit was a joke by the way.'

Debs smiled and stroked Liv's arm. 'I'm so sorry for that outburst. I should never have said that, Liv. I had no idea that you were so unhappy, hon. I've been so wrapped up in this holiday fling that I never noticed. I am *so*, *so* sorry.'

'What you see isn't always what's going on underneath. Yes, on the surface I have a perfect life, my husband throws money at me like I'm some lap dancer he met in a bar.' She mimicked him, '*Here you go, Liv, your chin is sagging a bit, go and have a face lift. Your tits are getting droopy, go and have a boob job!*'

'God, I wondered how your tits were so pert. I bloody knew it,' said Fiona.

They all burst into fits of giggles at Fiona's attempt to calm the situation. Tears streamed down both Liv's and Debs' faces, it wasn't clear whether from sadness or laughter.

'I have all the money I could ever want, I have

a fabulous house, but I have nothing for me. I've lost me. I don't know who I am any more. All I know is who I don't want to be. I want a job. I want to help people. I want to do something useful for others. I don't want to just potter about all day doing washing and ironing and walking the dog for something to do. I need to feel good about myself and right now I feel like shit.'

'Oh man, I had no idea, Liv. I'm so sorry,' said Debs again.

'And I'm sorry for what you've gone through. I wish you'd told us. I can't believe you went through that alone. Did Dave know?'

'No, it was in the early days. We'd been together a few months, then we split up and were having a break. I found out I was pregnant and didn't know what to do. So I made a decision that I've regretted for the rest of my life.'

'God, we've got some talking to do, haven't we? Perhaps it's a good job we've got some time on our hands right now.' They all held hands across the table in a big circle. 'We'll get through everything together. At least we have each other.' Liv squeezed Debs' hand.

'Martin, you got any more booze?' Debs asked.

'Now that is something I can definitely help you with.' He appeared with another bottle of bubbly. 'I really am sorry about everything tonight, ladies.'

'To be honest, Martin, getting stranded out here has probably given us a true opportunity to really talk and get a lot of things out in the open, so please don't worry. As long as the coastguard is on the way, we'll be fine. Won't we, girls?' Liv looked around at her friends and realised once again just how much she loved them.

Chapter Twenty-Eight

AMONGST MANY TEARS of laughter and sadness, and much talking, the chug of a motor could be heard as the coastguard veered around the headland towards them. A cheer went up from the friends, who were starting to shiver under their blankets. Raised voices in rapid-fire Portuguese that the ladies could not make out, and lots of arm flinging from everyone, eventually ceased and the coastguard clipped a bungee rope onto the back of the yacht and started to tow them back to land.

When the marina came into sight, another cheer was raised and holidaymakers looked to see where the noise was coming from. They just saw four women back from an evening's yacht trip. What they didn't see was that these friends had been sharing secrets that they'd kept bottled up for years. The old saying 'a problem shared is a problem halved' had held true. Every one of them felt lighter for getting worries off their chests and admitting concerns they'd been holding on to, which they really could, and should, have shared years ago.

As soon as they'd been able to get a phone signal, Liv had phoned ahead to the driver to pick them up and the car was waiting as they alighted the *Lady Marmalade*. Debs had sent a text to Eduardo, who must have been wondering where they were, arranging to meet him when they got back.

It was very quiet in the car on the short journey back to the villa, each of the women lost in their thoughts. When they arrived, Eduardo was leaning against the gate. His smile took Debs' breath away. She knew at that point what she was going to have to do and it wasn't going to be easy.

Exhaustion had taken over and Liv, Fiona and Samantha all went up to bed leaving Debs and Eduardo at the front door. They headed out to the terrace for five minutes peace and quiet where the moonlight shone onto the sea, making it glisten with sparkles.

'Have you had chance to think tonight, meu amor?'

'I've done nothing but think all evening,' she replied with a sad smile.

'Shall I let you go to bed? You look tired.'

'I would like to go to bed but only if you stay

with me again tonight. Our time together will come to an end soon and I want to wake up in your arms as many times as I can. Is that OK?'

'I could think of nothing more I'd rather do.' Eduardo led her by the hand upstairs.

WHEN SAMANTHA GOT to her room, she decided to send Peter a text message. She didn't care what time it was, if it woke him up, it woke him up. He probably wouldn't respond anyway.

Hello, darling. I have some things I need to talk to you about. Please let me know if you have any plans to come home in the next week or so, or if not, I'll come up to the uni and we can discuss them there. Love you always. Mum x.

She turned off her phone. She was so glad that she had choices to make in her life, some people weren't that lucky and illness cut their lives short. She was one of the fortunate ones and she was sure as hell going to make the most of every day ahead of her now that the cancer scare was behind her.

FIONA GOT HERSELF into her pyjamas and texted Brenda.

Hello. We've had quite a night. Got stranded on a boat trip, but all is OK and we're back home safely. Hope Mum is OK and I hope that you are too x

Within seconds her phone pinged.

Oh Fiona dear. I was just thinking about you. Marion is absolutely fine, eating well, making friends and having a lovely time. I hope you are. Really looking forward to seeing you when you are back. I know you have a late flight. Let me know what time you are coming to the home the following morning. I'll make sure I'm around x

As Fiona laid her head on her pillow, and started to drowse, she had no idea whether Brenda would end up being just a friend, or maybe more. But what she did know was that she was a very nice lady and Fiona hoped she would be in her life in one way or another.

LIV STUCK HER finger into the pot of moisturiser. The one thing she did every night without fail these days was to maintain a good skincare routine. As she gently patted her face and neck, letting the cream do its thing, and she thought about what she needed to do, it all suddenly slotted into place.

LAUGHTER GREETED DEBS and Liv as they sauntered into the lounge. Debs flung herself on the sofa next to Fiona and Samantha.

'You two sound happy.'

'We were just laughing about last night and about how you thought we were going to die out at sea.'

'Well, you do hear about sharks in Europe, you know. The boat could have sunk and we could have had to try to swim to safety.'

Fiona giggled again. 'Well, I'm glad we didn't. And thank you for being so understanding, about, well, everything.'

'Don't know why you didn't come clean about being a raging lezza years ago,' Debs said in her very unsubtle way. Fiona batted her on the arm and Debs grabbed her hand. 'We love you for being you. I hope you realise that now.' Fiona squeezed her hand back.

'Anyway, girls, we've been invited next door to Mikey's parents' villa this evening for food, and they've told us to dress up, so I'm going to lie on the terrace all day and top up my tan. Who's joining me?'

DETERMINED TO MAKE the most of their last day in Portugal, they spent their time relaxing by the pool, taking in the gorgeous views which they all knew they would never forget and eating a delicious lunch. It was so pleasant enjoying each other's company and chatting about what life had in store for them all when they got home.

At seven p.m. they knocked on the door of their neighbours' villa. Mikey and Bernardo met them and there were air kisses all round. Mikey looked so relaxed and happy. Eduardo was already in the lounge, looking very dapper in a navy-blue suit and an open-necked white shirt, and Keith and Angie stood to greet them. From nowhere a waiter appeared with a tray of full champagne flutes. These people really did know how to live in style.

'We hope it's OK with you ladies for us to dine outside on the terrace this evening?'

They all nodded. They'd only said earlier how they all loved the outdoor living aspect of the villa. So much time at home in the UK was spent indoors, and they all felt it was nice to be away and making the most of the warm weather and the open spaces.

'Shall we head out?' Keith waved them towards the doors.

To their complete surprise, the terrace was

decked in bunting and there were fairy lights everywhere with around a dozen silver balloons with 'Happy 50th Birthday' written all over them tied to every tree, chair and column of the pergola.

'Oh, look at what you've done! How lovely!' Liv put her hands to her mouth and squealed.

'Well, we couldn't have the four of you come out here to celebrate your fiftieth birthdays without some sort of proper celebration, now could we?' Angela smiled. 'Michael tells us you were together on your twenty-first birthdays too. Tell us about that.'

'Not sure we can. What happened in Corfu stays in Corfu.' Olivia winked at her.

'Well, we could maybe share some of it, not just all of it.' Debs laughed. 'And certainly not the bit about—'

'Come on, ladies, let's sit and let the men go and do men talk somewhere else. So, how have you enjoyed your holiday and your fiftieth birthday celebrations?' Angela asked. 'I bloody hated being fifty. We went out for a meal at a very expensive restaurant in London. It had been booked for nearly a year because it's so difficult to get a table. I had the worst hot flush of my life and spent most of the evening looking red and blotchy with my make-up sliding off my face, feeling like shit but putting a brave face on it for the rest of my family and friends. Most of those friends, I couldn't even remember their names because my brain cells seemed to have left my body and my memory is totally shocking. I'd have been happier staying at home in my flannelette pyjamas with a Chinese takeaway in front of the TV. How are you all coping with the menopause? Has it got any of you yet?'

Liv laughed and couldn't imagine this very glamorous lady in her cosies on the sofa at home. 'Well, I'm not too bad with the hot flushes but the constant rage that runs through my body for the most ridiculous reasons, and is totally uncontrollable, just confuses me. I yelled at a woman in the supermarket last week because she took the last of the fresh bread and I called her a selfish bitch. I couldn't believe I did it but at times everything and everyone really irritates me beyond words.'

'I'm so glad it's not just me,' said Samantha. 'It's the not sleeping that gets me. I wake up because I'm hot. It's not a hot flush, but since I hit fifty I think my body temperature has just increased in general. It's either that or the cavity wall insulation I had fitted last year. I fling a leg out from under the duvet, then the duvet is off completely, then back on because I'm freezing and by that stage I'm bloody wide awake. Especially when I also have to get up for a wee at least once in the night too. The amount of times I say to myself, Samantha, you need to go back to sleep because you've got to get up in a few hours. Then I may as well get up and make a cup of tea because I don't know what to do with myself. There's nothing worse than tossing and turning all night long and trying to force yourself to go back to sleep. I'm constantly tired, so I need a nap in the afternoon. I spend my whole weekend planning everything around the fact that I need a nap, which then means I can't sleep when I go to bed. It's a vicious circle. And not sleeping well is affecting my memory too! I go to say a sentence and can't bloody remember what word I wanted to use. I feel like an idiot. I wonder if I'm getting dementia! Oh, sorry, Fiona. I didn't mean...'

Fiona smiled at Samantha. 'Don't worry, hon. I know what you mean. It's something I worry about all the time too.'

'For me it's the fact that all of a sudden I can't control my bladder like I used to,' said Debs. 'And God only knows what might happen when I sneeze, cough or laugh these days. I have to concentrate that hard on clenching everything without trying to pull a face. I'm not sure what's going to come out of what orifice!'

Angela howled.

'It's a bloody nightmare. I'll be signing up to a monthly subscription with Tena Ladies soon.' Laughter erupted around the table. 'I just can't quite work out whether you can do a full-on wee in them, or if they're just there to mop up the dribbles.'

'Oh, Debs. Perhaps not something to share with the lovely Eduardo just yet, eh, sweetheart?'

'Honestly, don't make me laugh, Fiona. Anything could happen. It's as much a surprise to me as it is to everyone else.'

That made them all laugh even more.

'Goodness me. What's so funny?' Keith meandered over to the table to see what all the noise was about.

'Girl talk, darling, I'm sure you wouldn't be interested.' Angela swatted her husband away to go back to the men. 'Lucky bastards that they don't get what we get.'

'But they do have to put up with us, I suppose.'

They all started to giggle uncontrollably and Angela collared the waiter for more bubbly. 'Thank God for alcohol, is what I say. Cheers, ladies. Happy birthday.'

Josep came over to announce that dinner was

served and they all took their seats around the table.

On his way back to the kitchen, Josep beamed at Debs and whispered in her ear, 'You make my brother so happy, and that makes me happy. Thank you.'

He squeezed her shoulder and she smiled. He patted Eduardo on the back as he walked past. Her friends looked at her across the table and Liv thought Debs had never looked more beautiful than she did this evening, smiling at the man on her right, who was holding her hand under the table.

The huge marble table was very quickly filled with dishes containing salads, lobster and langoustines, chicken and vegetable kebabs, and paella; the smell of garlic and spices wafting into the evening air made them all realise how hungry that they were. The wine flowed freely and the evening continued to be delightful. Friends old and new, chatting about their pasts and their futures.

MIKEY STOOD AND announced that he'd like to say a few words.

'This has been a week I will never forget. To my parents, I just want to say a huge thank you for accepting Bernardo and I as a couple. You are wonderful parents and I love you very much. I hope that you come and spend many more holidays out here with us. I've absolutely adored spending time with you this week, now you know everything and we've not had to hide. Thank you. I'd like you all to raise your glasses to Keith and Angela. Cheers.'

Glasses clinked all around.

'I haven't finished yet!'

They all laughed. Bernardo gazed at Mikey adoringly.

'A week ago, I didn't know you ladies, yet now I feel like I've known you all my life. You've taken me into your hearts, and you've made friends with my parents. I've seen you all grow and flourish before my very eyes this week, and it's been a delight to be around you. I hope you will remember this holiday fondly and I hope you don't leave it too long before you come back to Portugal to see us. I'd like to wish you all a very happy fiftieth birthday. Here's to you, ladies.'

A huge chorus of cheers went around and many more clinking of glasses and lots of thank yous were shouted to him. He really was a superstar. He'd arranged this whole holiday and nothing had been too much trouble. Liv knew there were lots of her husband's friends who would definitely want to use a service like the one Mikey and Bernardo offered, and she knew that she'd be recommending them to anyone who would listen. She'd be raving about them when she got home.

At the thought of the word 'home', she grabbed her glass and knocked back what was left in it. The waiter appeared, as if in stealth mode, to refill it and she pushed all thoughts of home to the back of her mind as she continued to enjoy a perfectly wonderful evening with her friends.

Josep carried a huge birthday cake with literally fifty candles on it over to the table and insisted that all four ladies blew out the candles at the same time and made a wish. Each of them closed their eyes and made a secret wish and when they opened them there were hugs all around. Josep cut the cake and even though they thought that they couldn't eat another thing, they managed pretty well before they all stumbled back to their own villa, slightly worse for wear, giggling and wobbling, and all flinging their shoes off in the hallway before making their way to their respective rooms. Eduardo chased Debs up the stairs and they all fell about laughing.

Tomorrow was a huge day for them all. Packing to do, tidying up and they would go over all their plans again over breakfast, repeating them, and making a pledge to each other to go through with everything they had decided on over the last week to make their new dreams happen. This holiday had been wonderful and totally and utterly life-changing for each of them. Their new lives were just about to begin.

WHEN DEBS AND Eduardo got up to her room, she became serious and took his hand in hers. 'We need to talk.' It had been playing on her mind all day.

'You do know that I'm fifty years old, don't you, Eduardo? My days of being able to have children are behind me. Should you not be with someone younger, who could give you children?'

'Meu amor, I may not be very clever, but yes, I do know this. I am not so far behind you. As I told you, I shall be fifty myself in a few years. And I have something that I need to tell you before you make your decision.' Debs went to speak, but he raised his finger to her lips. 'Sshh. This is hard. You must listen, not speak.' Debs gulped, not knowing what on earth he was going to tell her.

'I have a daughter. Sabina. She is seventeen. She lives in Faro with her mother, Louisa. Louisa and I were together for a short time before she fell in love with someone else. I discovered a few years later that she'd had a child and that the child was mine. Sabina was three when I met her for the first time and I fell head over heels in love with her.

'Sabina is beautiful and I adore her. She comes to stay with me occasionally. *You* need to know about *her* before you make your decision as to whether you will stay, because she is a big part of my life. I have told her about you and she'd like to meet you. How do you feel about meeting her in the morning? I know that you go home tomorrow, but I would very much like the two of you to meet.'

Debs was stunned. She turned and busied her hands, but didn't realise they were trembling until she went to spoon coffee into cups. She certainly wasn't expecting that. Margo hadn't mentioned anything about a daughter when they'd chatted, and she was surprised that it was the first time Eduardo had mentioned it too.

He placed his hands on her shoulders and turned her to face him. 'Talk to me, Debs. How you feel?'

'I'm just surprised. You hadn't mentioned this.'

'When was I to mention it? When we met in the garden. Good morning, my name is Eduardo and I have a daughter. Our time together is so precious, I did not know when to tell you. But you go home tomorrow. And you need to know. So I tell you now. She is in my life and if you are going to be in my life too, which I hope you are, then it is important you know.'

Debs nodded. 'I am surprised, but yes, I'd like to meet her. Can you bring her here in the morning?'

He pulled her towards him. 'Oh Deb-orah, you are amazing. I never believed that love at first sight is a thing, but now I do.'

She looked deep into his eyes.

'I love you, meu ameu,' he said.

She laid her head on his chest, feeling safe and very much loved.

'I love you too.'

LIV GRABBED HER phone from the bedside cabinet, where it had spent most of the holiday and texted her husband's number with a message she would never have imagined sending a week ago. Once it had gone, she breathed a sigh of relief. Next she texted Mikey and asked whether he was around in the morning because she needed his help. He responded straight away.

Get the coffee on, and I'll be round at nine.

She laid out her running gear on the chair in the corner of the room, knowing that she needed to be up and out early to be back in time to see Mikey. Their flight was at seven p.m., and she had a lot of things to organise before then.

LIV SAT ON the terrace, her hands getting warmer from hugging a mug of coffee, and watched another spectacular sunrise. The beautiful hues of yellow and gold blended with the early morning sky, becoming a deeper rich blue by the minute, casting a glow over the line where the sky met the sea. It made for the prettiest picture that she hoped she'd never forget. This was a pivotal moment in her life. Perhaps the *biggest* day of her life.

She managed to pull herself away once the sun was fully up. It was time for her run to keep her head clear. As she walked back into the lounge, she bumped into Eduardo, who had clearly crept down the stairs and was trying to sneak out with his shoes in his hands. She smiled at the thought that he was creeping around. She hadn't realised he'd stayed over. She was glad that Debs had spent her last night with both her friends and him. Neither one had made her make a choice.

Debs appeared behind him in her running gear.

'OK if I join you?'

'Of course.' Liv grinned.

Eduardo blew Debs a kiss, and waved goodbye to them both.

'See you later,' Debs whispered after him.

'You're becoming quite the runner, aren't you?' said Liv once Eduardo had driven off.

'I never thought I'd see the day where I said that I was enjoying running, and I'm not sure that I'll have the motivation and love it quite so much when I'm doing it on my own, but I shall have a damn good try. I've spent way too long feeling sorry for myself since Dave left me. It's time I started to look after myself *and* put me first.'

'I'm proud of you, hon. I really am.' Debs smiled back at her friend.

'Thank you. Have you had any more thoughts about what you're going to do, Liv?'

'I have, but I'm still trying to get my head around them right now. Do you mind if we don't talk about it yet? I'll tell you over breakfast.'

'Of course, darling. You know that whatever you decide that we're all here for you, don't you?'

'I do, and likewise. Whatever decision you make, you know we'll support you. I'm so lucky to have you guys in my life. Just think back to a week ago and how much all our lives have changed in just a short time. Quite amazing really.'

'It sure is. And Eduardo threw another spanner into the works last night.'

'Come on, let's run and you can tell me all about it on the way round.'

They walked out to the gate. Debs relayed the news about Eduardo's daughter from the previous evening. She'd got used to the idea but was still feeling quite nervous about meeting Sabina later that morning.

'What if she's rude to me? What if she clearly doesn't like me?'

'And what if she's the daughter that you never had? Have you thought about that at all?'

Debs stopped running and stared after Liv, who jogged on the spot.

'Sometimes you have to see the positives instead of the negatives in life. You could become great friends and she could fill a space that you never thought possible. How could she not love you? You're fucking fabulous. Come on, don't stop. You have to keep running.'

Debs joined Liv once more, her brain even more jumbled than it was before. What if Liv was right? Now wouldn't that be amazing. What should she wear? Should she put make-up on or go au naturel? Why did she overthink everything? She laughed at herself. She needed to lighten up.

Chapter Twenty-Nine

FARO AIRPORT WAS buzzing with activity; loved ones saying goodbye to each other, tourists at the end of their holidays, others just landed and traipsing through with cases, keen to take in the sights and sounds of the Algarve for however long they were staying. Mikey appeared, pushing a trolley loaded with cases while the ladies were looking for their flights back to their respective corners of the UK.

'You ladies don't believe in travelling light, do you?'

'It's all that extra stuff we bought at the market. We really love it here in Portugal, Mikey, and can so understand why you live here. Portugal will always have a special place in my heart and hopefully it won't be too long before we're back. Thank you for being the best organiser in the world.' Fiona kissed his cheek.

'Just don't mention the boat trip, please.' Nervous laughs all round signified the mood.

'Thank you, Fiona. And you need to remember to go and be yourself. Don't worry what the world thinks. Look at how much time I wasted worrying what people thought when I really didn't need to. Good luck with everything.'

Samantha turned and put both her hands on Mikey's shoulders. 'It's been wonderful, Mikey. Thank you for all that you've done to make this a holiday to remember. It's been so special. It really has.' She kissed both his cheeks. 'And I'm so glad you got everything sorted out too. I'm very happy for you.'

'Thank you, Samantha. I hope your new exciting life works out. Can't wait to hear all about it.'

He turned to Debs and Liv. 'Ready, ladies?'

There were nods, then kisses all round and even the odd tear as the four friends departed on the next stage of their lives, which they'd all worked out while there in the Algarve. This had certainly been a holiday none of them would forget.

MIKEY GOT INTO the passenger side of the car and told the driver they were ready to go. He turned to the back seat.

'Now, are you both absolutely sure?'

Debs and Liv held hands and looked each other deep in the eye and nodded in solidarity.

'We're sure.'

AS THE DRIVER headed back to the villa, Liv looked out the window of the limo and thought back to the events of the morning. Showering after her run had brought everything into focus. She'd had a word with Mikey and she'd learnt the villa was free for the next week, so she could stay there longer while she tried to work out everything. As she'd dried herself, she became more sure with each movement that the decision she had made was the right one.

Grabbing her phone from the bedside cabinet, she had dialled George's number. It diverted to answerphone, so she ended the call. Two minutes later she picked it up again and plucked up the courage to leave a message.

'George, I'm so sorry but I can't come home today. You've probably not even noticed, but I've been extremely unhappy for a while. I'm going to stay out here in Portugal for a little longer while I work out what I want to do long term. I miss our old life, George. I don't like this new one. In fact, I hate it. That's why I need some time to work out what I want. I'm sorry. I do love you all, but I miss being your wife and a mum to the boys, rather than someone who is treated like a member of the household staff. I just can't come home right now. Bye.' Her voice cracked on that last word. She'd been trying so hard to stay strong but the enormousness of what she'd done hit her by the end.

She doused her face with cold water to try to hide her red eyes. She headed downstairs and there was a knock at the door. Eduardo and a pretty young lady stood on the other side, both looking apprehensive.

'Come in, come in. You must be Sabina. It's so nice to meet you.'

Sabina took her hand and Eduardo kissed her cheek.

'Thank you, Olivia.' He looked very nervous.

AS THEY WALKED into the lounge Debs stood and walked over to Sabina first and held out both hands to her. Sabina hesitated. Everyone was watching and seemed to be holding their breath. Sabina took Debs' hands and smiled at the woman standing before her who was smiling back. It felt as if one big breath was exhaled from each of them.

A nervous, high-pitched giggle escaped Sabina's lips. 'I am so pleased to meet the lady who make my papa so happy.' She beamed and her face lit up just like her father's did when he looked at Debs.

Debs' heart filled with such joy she thought it might burst. Her eyes teared up.

'Why don't you all go out to the terrace and I'll make some drinks,' said Liv.

She headed through to the kitchen. Eduardo said he was going to check on the garden, leaving Debs and Sabina alone. Debs had never felt so tense in her life. Sabina may have been young, but Debs could see she had spirit and she immediately liked her. But she was completely tongue-tied right now – all the things she had rehearsed to say to Sabina when they met went straight from her brain and she had no idea what to say.

'Sabina—'

'Deb-orah—'

'No, you first.' Debs smiled at this beautiful young lady in front of her.

'Thank you. I just want to say I am so very pleased that Papa find someone to make him happy. He work all day, and is alone at night. I worry about it. He tell me that you make his heart fill with joy and that make me happy too.' She smiled again. 'Papa tell me that he ask you to stay here? Have you made a decision yet?'

'To be honest with you, Sabina, I was waiting to meet you. I don't have children of my own. I wasn't able to. But I know how important children are to a parent and I would *never* want to come between a father and his daughter. I wanted to see how you felt about it. It's all been very quick.' Her voice quivered.

'We've only just met, Deb-orah.' Debs smiled at the way she said her name exactly the same way her father did when he first met her. 'But I like you, and I would like to get to know you better. I know that things are complicated and you have a lot to work out, but love isn't in your head. Love is in your heart and it's how you feel. Papa is a very good, how you say, judge of character?' Debs nodded thinking that this young lady was wise beyond her years. 'And if he like you very much, then I think that I will like you too. Perhaps we could spend time alone together. And then the three of us spend time together. Today families come in all shapes and sizes. And when I'm not with Papa, I would like to think that he is not alone and has someone to love him and look after him. He does need a bit of looking after. After all he is a man. And sometimes they can be very stupid.' She grinned and Debs realised she wanted to get to know this young lady more.

'I would like that very much, Sabina.'

'Then I think you need to go tell Papa your decision and put him out of his miserable.'

Debs laughed through her tears. She headed outside to Eduardo, who was pruning a tree. He wrinkled his brow when he saw her approaching, his eyes questioning what was going to come next. She leaned up, kissed his cheek, took the secateurs from his hand and placed them on the nearby wall, then took both of his hands in hers. She looked down at the floor, before lifting her eyes to his.

'Eduardo! If you still want me, then I'm yours.'

'Oh, Debs. You are going to stay?'

Debs nodded, never more sure of anything in the world. 'I'll have to go back at some point to get some stuff and to work out what to do with the house, but yes, I'd really like to stay with you.'

Before she knew it, she was lifted from the ground by a pair of big strong arms and twirled around, her face being covered in what felt like a million tender kisses. Laughter erupted from her.

'I am the happiest man in the world. I am so excited about our future.'

Sabina walked out towards them.

'Sabina, Sabina, she said yes!' her father shouted across the garden.

Debs opened up her arms to Sabina and she joined the embrace. All Debs needed to do now, was to work out how it was all going to happen.

Chapter Thirty

LIV WAS STILL thinking about the huge decision she had made only this morning. Samantha and Fiona were on their way home, and Eduardo, Debs and Sabina had gone into Vilamoura for a celebratory early meal and to talk about their plans for the future. Debs needed to work out when to go back to the UK, hand in her notice at work, what to do with the house. She should probably tell Dave her plans, too, even though it was really nothing to do with him. Liv had asked if they would mind if she stayed back at the villa. She had a lot of thinking to do.

She knew she loved her family, always had and always would, but she wanted to feel valuable in their lives. She wanted her opinion to matter, her views to be taken into consideration. She wanted them to ask her how she felt about certain things. She knew she'd made a rod for her own back by pandering to their every whim, but it had seemed easier when they boys were younger. Now they just took her totally and utterly for granted.

When she heard a knock on the villa's door, she ambled to the foyer expecting it to be Mikey checking up on her. He'd said earlier that he'd pop in to see how she was. But to her total shock, there – standing on the doorstep when she opened the door – was someone she had never expected.

'Olivia. Oh my God. Are you OK?'

'George, what a surprise. Of course I'm OK. Where are the boys?'

'My mother is looking after them. When I got your message, I packed a few things and I headed for the airport while Cynthia booked the next possible flight. I want to know what I can do to sort everything out. Olivia, you have to tell me what is going on. I've never been so shocked by anything in my life. I thought you were happy.'

'You'd better come in.'

He shut the door behind him, and turned to look around him, taking in the splendour of the beautiful villa. 'Wow! This is stunning.'

'It is. Come and have a look out the back. The view is amazing. Do you remember when we were first married, George? We always talked about having a holiday home in Portugal.'

'So we did. I'd forgotten all about that.'

Liv raised an eyebrow, which didn't go unnoticed by her husband. She walked through to the kitchen area and held up the kettle.

'Coffee or wine?'

He pointed to the wine. 'I think if we've got some sorting out to do. We should perhaps do it over a glass or two of vino.'

She smiled back at him.

'God, Olivia. I've been such a fool. Life has been so manic in the business, and I think it's taken over my life. I've forgotten all about those early dreams we had. There was so much we wanted to do together. We had so many hopes for the future. We wanted to see the world, take on the world. I've been thinking on the plane on the way over. I really don't know what I'd do without you, Olivia. I really do hope that we can sort whatever this is out.'

Olivia sipped at her wine. Right now she couldn't trust herself to speak. Her heart was hammering in her chest. She walked around George and sat on the sofa, tucking her knees beneath her.

'You look beautiful, you know. But then, to me you always do.'

'Do I?'

'Of course. You know I think that. Don't you?'

She shook her head.

'You always look amazing, Olivia. You're as beautiful now as you were the day I met you.'

'How can I know that, George, when you never tell me? Our life is such a rush. You spend most weekends in the golf club, and I have to come and pick you up, so we're always rushing to get ready to go out. I honestly cannot remember the last time you told me I looked nice in something. When we were first married we used to spend hours getting ready to go out together. You used to lie on the bed and watch me try on lots of different dresses, telling me I looked fabulous in them all. You couldn't keep your hands off me, George.'

'But, Olivia, life gets in the way.'

'Life gets in the way if you let it, George. Marriage and parenthood aren't easy. There's no handbook that comes with them, either. We should pull together and do things as a family, not as two people living in the same house. Or even four people. Especially when one of those people is trying to balance it all like a deck of cards, wondering just when the hell it is going to topple over.'

'I had no idea you felt like this.'

'And why would you? We barely spend time together. If you're not at work, you are in the golf club or at some charity event. And if I'm not in the house, I'm running around getting the boys to whichever classes they need to be at, and doing the washing and ironing of their rugby kits, their football kits, their karate outfits, their school uniforms. It's like a never-ending hamster wheel. And I hate it. I hate my life.'

There, she'd said it to his face.

'I honestly had no idea you were feeling this way. We struggled so hard at the start of our married life together, in the place that we called home then. I thought that if you had the money to do anything you wanted, that you'd be happy. I've got it all so wrong, haven't I?'

Liv nodded at him. 'Yes,' she whispered.

He closed the gap between them on the sofa. Their knees were touching and he took her hands in his. 'What are we going to do, darling? Tell me what you want me to do and I'll put it right. I'll do anything. Please.'

She looked at the man before her. He was the man whose eyes she had met across a crowded dance floor at her twenty-third birthday party. The man who had swept her off her feet, treating her like a princess. The man with whom she had stood in front of a vicar in their village church nearly twenty-five years ago and vowed to love until the day she died. He was the father of her two children. He was once her everything. But was he all of that now?

She heard his belly rumble and knew he must be hungry. He probably hadn't had anything for a while. She went to offer to get him some food, but then changed her mind. It was this servant-like habit she'd got herself into that was making her feel this way.

'There's some food in the fridge, if you'd like to help yourself.'

'Thank you, but right now I'm too scared to eat. I'm scared of what you are going to say to me, Olivia.'

'You should eat, George. I need some time to think. You've totally thrown me by turning up here like this. How did you even know where I was?'

'Ah well, don't shout at me, but I went through your emails. I tried the boys' names for your password, then when I came up blank Seb suggested I try the dog's name. Bingo.'

'My darling Hector. How is he?'

'He's pining for you! He just sits by the door looking forlorn and every time he hears a movement, he's dancing on all four paws, hoping it's you. And when it's not he goes back to looking sad and puts his head on his paws, staring at me with those big brown eyes.'

'Ah, my sweetheart. I do miss him. I've missed running with him.'

'What can I do, Olivia? Please tell me it's not too late for us. I'll do anything.'

He stared deep into her eyes and she wondered whether he'd been taking lessons from Hector.

'I want to start my own business, George.'

'We can do that. I can look around for something and I can buy you a going concern. Get you some staff. Job's a good 'un!'

'You're missing the point totally, George. I want to do this for myself. You can't fix everything by throwing money at it, you know.'

George looked devastated. 'Olivia, I work damn hard so that you and the boys can have everything you want. Damn hard.'

'You do, George. I'm not disputing that. But this is something I want to do. I might need to ask for your advice, but I need to do it for myself.'

She explained her business idea and he nodded at her. She reached over into her handbag and got out a notebook. She ran through her ideas.

'You really have been doing some thinking, haven't you?'

'It's got my brain working again, George. Not just about what needs washing for what day, and who needs to be at what club and at what time. This has truly got my mind working. And it's exciting me. I can't honestly remember the last time I was excited about doing something.

'Remember when you first started the business and we'd sit at night and work out how to make things better and run more smoothly? I used to help you then, but for some reason you stopped asking me. I miss those days. I miss being part of what you do. The only time I'm involved in the company is when you are entertaining and want to show off the house and your family.'

'That's a bit unfair. I'm proud of what we've achieved and the things that we've got.'

'But I'd swap them all tomorrow to have my old George back. Not the show-offy George who wants to be better than everyone else. Just good old humble, hard-working George, who loves his family and puts them first.'

George gulped. 'I thought it was what you wanted. You've never gone without a thing.'

'The only thing I ever wanted, George, was you. You and the boys. Remember when they were young and on a Saturday night we used to sit and have a takeaway and watch *X-Factor*? A proper family night. We had three sofas in the lounge and we all used to sit on the same one, snuggling up with each other. Now, we're lucky to all be in the same room. The boys sit in their rooms playing on their electronic games, and if they are in the same room as us, you and they are always on phones or iPads. I miss us being a family.'

George poured more wine. 'I think it's going to be a long night. But there is nothing that you've said to me so far that I don't think we can fix. Do you feel the same? Do you want to fix things? Oh, Olivia,' his voice quivered. 'I love you so much. We all do and we want you home.'

Olivia reached out and stroked his cheek. Stubble was starting to come through, and he wasn't looking like the smooth-shaven husband who left the house early each morning. She looked deep into his eyes.

'Do you want me home, or do you *need* me home, George? They're two very different things.'

'I very much want you home, Olivia. I have never once in all of our years together ever looked at another woman. I've never needed to. I've had everything I've ever wanted in you. You are beautiful, you are bright, you are kind, you are an amazing mother to our boys and you are my everything. I adore you, and I've clearly been pretty bloody shitty at showing you that. Please let me try to make it up to you and make everything better. Please say you'll give me a chance and I promise I won't let you down.'

Olivia yawned and stretched her arms above her head. She was shattered. Getting all of this out tonight had been cathartic yet exhausting. These were things she'd been bottling up for a very long time.

George put his head in his hands and his shoulders started to shake. Her touch on his back made him look up and she looked deep into his eyes and remembered just how very much she loved this man before her.

'Do you want me to find a hotel to book into? I didn't even think of organising anywhere. I just wanted to come straight here to you.'

'No, George. Stay here.'

'Are you sure?'

'I'm absolutely sure. There's no place I'd rather you be.'

She took her husband by the hand and led him to her bedroom and showed him exactly how sure she was.

LIV HAD SLEPT more soundly than she had for weeks. The next morning, she stretched and yawned as she sauntered downstairs in her dressing gown to the smell of bacon and eggs cooking in the kitchen and her husband singing and dancing around the kitchen in his boxer shorts and an apron. She raised her eyebrows. It had been a very long time since she had seen a sight like this.

'A full English for my wifey!' He planted a kiss on her nose as she gazed at him in astonishment and he placed her plate on the table, leading her by the arm to the chair.

She honestly couldn't remember the last time he had cooked anything.

'I've still got it, you know.' He winked at her as he fetched his own plate from the work surface.

There was nothing nicer than someone else cooking for you. She always felt things took so long to prepare and cook that when she sat down she couldn't really be bothered to eat. He'd even remembered how she liked her eggs. It was delicious and she ate the lot.

'Coffee, senhora?'

'Good grief!' She looked around her in feigned shock. 'Call the police. Someone's taken my husband away and replaced him with an imposter!'

He clutched his hand to his heart. 'Oh, that hurts! What you will find, my love, is today is the first day of the rest of our lives. I've spoken with my mother and she's happy to have the kids for a little while longer, and suggested you and I spend some time together out here. It's been a while since we had a holiday and it's been over fourteen years since we had a holiday on our own. So how about it, wifey?' He leant on his elbow and fluttered his eyelashes at her dramatically.

She loved him calling her 'wifey'. When they were first married he called her nothing else. It was another one of those things that had dwindled away over the years. It sounded good. She looked at the man in front of her and couldn't believe she had even considered throwing everything that they had away.

'I think it sounds absolutely wonderful. But without wishing to put a dampener on things, one full English and a pot of coffee isn't going to mend everything.'

'I absolutely know that, darling, and that's why I think it's a good idea for us to spend some time together out here and work out exactly how we're going to do things differently in the future. But anything you want, you've got it. If you want the cleaner to do more hours, then we'll arrange it. If you want me to take on more of the stuff at home, let's work out a rota and we'll start it as soon as we get back. Whatever it takes. I swear to you that I'm committed to you and that I'm prepared to do the work.

'And, also, we've got a lot of talking to do about your business idea. If you want my help, then I'm very happy to give it to you, but if you don't, then I'll let you get on with it. But I would like to be involved if you'd let me. Just remember how good we used to be when we put our heads together.'

George went to pick up her plate to take it over to the sink, but Liv grabbed his hand as he was passing. She pulled him close to her and he leant down and took her in his arms. She breathed him in. Her George. Her husband. The love of her life. And she knew in that moment, that whatever the future held for them, it was going to be together, and everything was going to work out OK.

'MUM, MUM!'

Olivia turned to see her sons hurtling towards her. Seb flung his arms around her waist and squeezed her tightly, and James pulled her into his shoulder. At fourteen he towered over her.

'I've missed you, Mum,' he whispered into her ear.

She took a huge breath. God, how could she possibly have forgotten how much she loved these boys? How could she have even thought about causing devastation in their lives by splitting up their family? She clung onto them both as tightly as she could.

'You can let go now, Mum.' James grinned at her.

'I'm never letting go of my mummy again. Please don't go away again, Mum. It's been awful,' said Seb.

She laughed at the dismay on his face when she ruffled his hair. 'Don't worry, mate. I'm back now. And I know I've not been away for that long, but you've both grown. I'm sure of it.'

'That's because Grandma has been making us eat loads of vegetables. She'd given so much cabbage and broccoli to us that we gave it to the dog when she wasn't looking and he keeps farting all the time and scaring himself.'

Liv laughed at the thought. She couldn't wait to see Hector.

'Well, I hope you've been behaving for your grandma if she's been good enough to look after you.'

Liv and her mother-in-law had never been the best of friends. She was one of those mothers who'd never really wanted her child to leave home and still treated George like he was about ten every time they went to visit. Liv felt she was never good enough for Kathleen and that she always looked down her nose at her. She was old school, and believed that women stayed at home looking after the house and the children, and had meat and two veg on the table for when their man came home from work.

While they'd been away, Olivia and George had talked lots and admitted that they didn't communicate well with each other these days. George had thought that giving her money so she could buy whatever she wanted made her happy. In fairness, she'd never told him that it didn't. She hadn't wanted to offend him. They made a pact that if either of them was not totally happy about something, that they had to have a conversation about it. It was all about communication.

Grandma Kathleen appeared from the coffee shop, where she'd been watching their arrival. Greeting her daughter-in-law, she put both hands on her shoulders.

'Olivia, darling. You look all sun-kissed and fabulous.' She pulled her into her ample bosom and hugged her tightly. Liv couldn't remember her ever doing this before in all her married life.

Kathleen kissed her son on his cheek and gave him the keys to the Range Rover. She tucked

Olivia's hand into the crook of her arm. Olivia turned around to make sure the boys were following her. James flicked Seb on his face and Seb cried out, 'Muuuum, tell him!'

She spoke at the same time as her husband. 'James—'

'That's enough, James. Leave your brother alone. NOW!'

Olivia quite liked this assertive side to her husband. Normally he left the disciplining of the children to her, and she really did hope that he had turned a corner and that this wasn't going to be something that was short-lived. Although she knew that if she wanted to keep her family together, she wasn't going to let it. She would do everything in her power to make it all work out, to help them work things out together.

'Boys, come with me and we'll go grab the car. You two can wait here and I'll text you when I'm in the waiting area,' said George.

This was a little different to the last time they went on holiday, when George was texting someone from work on his phone while she battled to put the cases in the car, pay the parking ticket and get the children to stop bickering with each other. He really did seem to be turning over a new leaf.

Kathleen smiled at her. 'Darling, you deserve a bloody medal. If I had to put up with your family twenty-four hours a day, I'd be buggering off to Portugal on a one-way ticket. They're bloody horrendous! How on earth do you cope with them? It's been lovely to see them all, but dear God, I can't wait to get home. I'm exhausted!' She winked and the two women laughed in solidarity.

'I hope you don't mind but I've taught the boys, and I include the big one in that, how to use the washing machine and tumble dryer. I've taught the smaller two, who, by the way, are actually growing every day and have eaten us out of house and home, that they need to pick up their dirty pants off the floor and put them into their laundry baskets and that anything else on the floor that doesn't belong there, probably needs to go into the bin. I've taught them a few other things too, so I hope they'll show you when you get home.'

'Thank you so much. It's my own fault, Kathleen. I've done everything for them over the years. It just seemed quicker and less trouble. If I did everything I didn't have to face the grumpy faces and mardy responses.'

'And what's George's excuse?'

'Again, I think I just wanted to give him what he wanted. To make him feel like he was king of his castle. But I've probably made my whole family ungrateful and unhelpful by not teaching them the right way.'

'There is no right or wrong way though, darling. There's no rule book when you become a parent and a wife. You just have to muddle through to the best of your abilities. I have an apology to make to you too. I'm sorry I've not been more supportive over the years. I wish I'd seen what was happening and if I'd been around more, I would have. I'd have seen that George wasn't pulling his weight at home and if I'd have made more of an effort to see you, I would have seen that you weren't happy. Let's not be strangers any more, Olivia. Despite them being a nightmare to look after, I've really enjoyed spending time with them all. I want to be more of a part of all your lives, if you'll allow me to be.'

'I would love that, Kathleen.'

'I left George's father once a long time ago, you know.'

Liv didn't think she'd ever been so shocked in her life. 'Really? George never said.'

'George never knew and I would never tell him. Please do keep this to yourself. I was feeling exactly the same way as you did. I never went as far as getting on a flight to Portugal, though I did pack a bag, leave a note on the kitchen table and walk out when he was at work one day. George was at school. I was totally and utterly exhausted and I didn't know what to do with myself. I was tired of not being me, of being a wife and a mother, with no time for anything else. I caught the bus into town and bumped into someone I used to work with. She told me her husband had had a heart attack and had passed away and she was so deeply sad and on her own, bravely bringing up her two small children. I felt like such an ungrateful madam and a complete and utter fool, so I came home. I threw away the note in the wastepaper bin, unpacked my case and went on with my day.'

'Oh my goodness, Kathleen. Did he ever know?'

'I never said anything to him, but when I went into the kitchen that evening, the note had been taken out of the bin and ripped into tiny pieces and sat on the windowsill. Tom came in, picked them up and took them into the garden where he struck a match and set fire to the shreds. He came back in, gave me a kiss, told me he loved me more than anything in his life and said he was sorry that he'd let me down. We *never* spoke about it again.

'Sometimes our men need a short sharp shock

to kick them into shape. They're a bit stupid, you see, and need everything pointed out to them. They go from one extreme to the other. They want to be the head of their family, but you still have to remind them to put on their socks and pants in the morning, or who knows how they'd be dressed.'

Liv smirked.

'If you want a man to do something, you have to act helpless and ask them to do it. They feel like a big man helping out their family and everyone's happy. It's just a big game. But he also needs to know that he needs to make you happy too. It's a shame he didn't realise buying you lots of stuff wasn't making you happy. Just keep talking to each other, darling, and if you need a friend, you know you can pick up the phone to me. Anytime. And I really do mean that, from the bottom of my heart.'

If this offer had come before she'd been away with the girls, Olivia might have dug her heels in and not bothered with Kathleen, but she felt more mellow since she'd mulled things over and wanted to look forward not backwards. Life was too short, and not forgiving someone did as much damage to yourself as them.

'And if you ever feel like running away to the sun again, for Christ's sake give me a ring and I'll be there as fast as I can throw some knickers and a toothbrush in my handbag!'

Liv grinned and hugged Kathleen tightly. 'Thank you for everything,' she whispered into her hair.

'To be honest, I don't think you'll need to do it ever again. You've scared the living daylights out of George. If there's anything you want him to buy you right now – new car, new designer bag or shoes – I'd ask away, because I think he'd give you the world to stop you leaving him. He was petrified.'

'I don't want the world, Kathleen. I just want my husband back.'

'I know. And I think you might just be in luck.'

This was the most affection the two women had ever shown to each other and Liv hoped that it was the start of a blossoming friendship that they'd been missing out on for years.

The bleep of a text on Kathleen's phone signified that the boys were outside.

'Come on, sweetheart, let's get you home.'

Chapter Thirty-One

LIV WAS GLAD it felt great to be home, she hadn't been sure how she'd feel. As she peered around the kitchen door, Hector spotted her and came bounding across the room, nearly knocking her over.

'Steady on, boy!' she laughed. 'Have you missed me?'

He jumped up and put his paws on her shoulders and licked her. He had such a smiley face and he looked absolutely thrilled to see her. He hopped around on all four paws and she nearly tripped over him as he got under her feet as she made her way over to the kettle.

'Mum, stay where you are. *I* am going to make you a cuppa.'

'Wow, Seb. Are you sure?'

'I'm absolutely sure! Grandma showed me how. She told me I had to do it for you when you got home.'

'You weren't supposed to tell her that bit

though, you muppet!' James lightly cuffed his younger brother on the back of his head and they laughed at each other.

It was nice that they were laughing instead of shouting. She looked across at George, and he smiled back at her.

Her kitchen was filled with everything and everyone she loved. Her heart was full of joy and she couldn't believe quite how close she had come to throwing it all away. She was looking forward to tomorrow, when she could start to concentrate on her business idea and getting it off the ground. She was excited about the future once more and grateful for her friends. Her friends that gave her the space to work out what she needed to, were there to listen when she needed them and who would always be close to her heart.

SAMANTHA SLAMMED HER front door closed, kicking the post that had gathered behind it out of the way, and wondered why the landing light was on. She was sure she hadn't left it on when she left a week ago. Wow. Was it really only a week since she flew out to Portugal? She heard a creak on the landing, and immediately she knew she wasn't alone. Her heart started to pound.

'Helloooo. Who is there?' Her voice was shaking. Dear God, please don't let there be burglars in the house.

She picked up an umbrella from the coat stand in the hall and started to creep her way upstairs. 'Who's there?'

Her heart was beating hard as the bathroom door started to move. She closed her eyes, flicked the umbrella catch so it opened, and launched herself at the figure in the doorway and screamed, '*Get out of my house, you thieving bastard!*'

'Fuck's sake, Mum. What the hell are you doing, you weirdo?'

'Peter. OMG! You nearly gave me a heart attack.' Her six-foot-two-inches tall son stood in front of her with a towel wrapped around his middle.

'What are you doing here?'

'Well, that's a delightful welcome home, isn't it?' He grinned at his mum. 'You said you needed me to come home because you needed to talk to me, and I have some stuff to say too, so I thought I'd be here for when you got back.'

'But why was the house in darkness?'

'I've just had a shower. Oh, how I've missed our power shower. The water in the one in our flat just trickles out and isn't always hot depending on who has been in before you! And I don't even want to think about the hair round the plughole! I didn't realise it had gone dark outside. Sorry, Mum, I didn't mean to scare you. I wasn't sure what time you were coming back. You just said tonight. Come here.'

Peter wrapped his big strong arms around his mum, and she breathed in the scent of him. A scent she'd missed so much since he'd been away. She didn't know how to react to this man-boy before her. He was still so much her little boy that she wanted to cradle to her chest, but physically he was a man and he was doing the cradling. She didn't want to scare him away, but she also wanted to hold him tight and never let him go.

'I've really missed you, Mum. I'm not sure I realised just how much until I came back. I tried so hard to be independent and not call you all the time, even though after a week all I wanted to do was pack up my stuff and come home to you. I'm sorry if that meant I didn't call at all, but I couldn't risk it. I knew that if I called you, you'd hear it in my voice and you'd tell me to come home. I couldn't put that burden on you and I didn't want you to worry. You always knew what I was thinking, normally before I did.'

These were more words than she'd heard him

speak in months. When he'd gone away to uni originally, he was really quiet. She hadn't wanted to tell him how much she was going to miss him, because she hadn't wanted to make it a huge thing. She was devastated when the night before he went away, she'd cooked him a lovely tea, his favourite meat pie, mash and veg, and the minute he'd eaten it, he'd gone out to meet his friends. She thought that they'd spend their last evening together and was gutted when he didn't seem to see the importance of the occasion.

The following day, when she took him to his halls of residence and got him settled in, in the half-hour slot they were given, she felt he couldn't wait to get rid of her. He'd booked an event for that lunchtime so he could meet some people and he was desperate to go off to that.

That Christmas, when he came home, he didn't say a lot about uni, although he did say how he was getting on well with the people in his flat but spent most of his time in his room, on his Xbox. When he went back in the new year, he was just as quiet. While she thought that he was quietly leaving her, and starting a life without her in it, he was clearly having his own struggles and couldn't voice them, not even to his mother.

He gave her that boyish grin that had always

wrapped her around his little finger and she knew that everything was going to be OK. It was silly to forget that most things in life were about communication. If people talked more, they'd know what each other were thinking, rather than assuming the wrong thing. There was probably nothing in the world that couldn't be sorted out with better communication. World wars, famine, politics. People just needed to talk.

All Samantha and Peter needed to do was to find their new normal. They'd done it before when Robert had died and they'd muddled through that time. But right now, she was simply going to enjoy every minute of her boy being home.

'Come on, son, let's go and get some supper sorted out. I bet you've been living on beans on toast, haven't you?'

Peter grinned. 'I've missed your cooking, Mum.' He sat at the kitchen table. 'And I'm sorry I've been an arse.'

She walked behind him and rested her head on his and placed her hands on his shoulders. She kissed his head. 'You have, but I still love you.'

They both laughed and she knew everything was going to be OK.

FIONA DROVE STRAIGHT to the care home from the airport. She'd rung Brenda on the way, and she'd said that she'd be there waiting for her. Fiona couldn't wait to see her mum. While it had been a relief to take a break, she'd missed her mum terribly.

Brenda met her at the entrance and gave her a hug. She was looking pretty in jeans and a cornflower-blue jumper, which brought out the colour of her eyes much more than the normal uniform she wore.

'It's good to see you, Fiona.'

'It's good to see you too, Brenda. How is she tonight?'

'She's in great spirits. I think you'll be pleasantly surprised.'

Fiona knocked on the door of her mum's room and heard a weak, 'Come in.'

Her mum was sitting up in bed, propped up on lots of pillows, gazing at a painting on the wall. It looked as if she'd had her hair done recently, and she had colour in her cheeks. Fiona was amazed at how well she looked and she gave a sigh of relief.

'Hello, Mum,' Fiona whispered.

She never knew what reaction those words could get. Most of the time, it was pure confusion.

Her mum turned her heard towards the voice,

and at first looked puzzled. 'Fiona? Is that you, Fiona?'

There was a huge lump in Fiona's throat. She remembered her.

'Is that really you, dear? Come here where I can see you better.'

'Yes it's me, Mum. I've been on holiday.'

'I know that, silly. And you look lovely, all tanned and pretty. You've been off to Portugal with your friends for the week, haven't you?'

Fiona laughed and a sob caught in her breath as well. 'Yes I have, Mum. I didn't know if you would remember.'

'I might be old, but I'm not daft. As if I'd ever forget that. Come and sit beside me on the bed.' She patted the space next to her.

Fiona squeezed into the space on the bed facing her mum. She seemed to have filled out a bit since the last time she'd seen her. Having someone feed her at the right times, and make sure she was eating it, was obviously doing her the world of good. While Fiona tried so hard, she couldn't be with her mum every minute of every day, and sometimes she'd make her mum a sandwich and come back, and it wasn't eaten. When she tried to cajole her mum to eat, she got angry and told her to stop telling her what to do. But that woman seemed a million miles away from the woman sitting in front of her right now.

Her mum took her hand and kissed it. She reached out and stroked her face. 'My beautiful daughter. My beautiful Fiona. I do love you, my darling.'

The lump in Fiona's throat was getting bigger than ever and a tear was forming in her left eye, which she tried to blink away. This was the first time in months her mum had remembered who she was and the first time in a very long time she'd told her she loved her. Those words meant everything to Fiona. It didn't matter that sometimes her mum got confused. All she knew in her heart was that in that very moment her mother knew who she was and she loved her, and her heart fell full of joy.

She looked up at Brenda in the doorway and smiled. She mouthed 'thank you' at her. Brenda smiled back.

Marion looked away at the painting on the wall and then again at her daughter. She frowned. 'What are you doing sitting on my bed? Have you come to bring my cup of hot chocolate, nurse?'

Fiona giggled. 'Yes I have, Marion. I'll just go and get it for you.'

Brenda gave her a hug as she walked out. 'She's

doing really well. I told you we'd look after her, didn't I?'

'You did, Brenda, thank you!'

Brenda linked arms with Fiona. 'Come on, let's go and make Marion that hot chocolate and you can tell me all about your holiday.'

DEBS STEPPED OUT onto the balcony overlooking the bay at Eduardo's house. Lights twinkled in the distance to show that the nearby town was still wide awake, and the huge full moon cast a light that shimmered prettily on the water. Footsteps behind her let her know she wasn't alone. Arms snaked around her waist and the warm breath on her neck made her shiver.

'I hope you are not having regrets, my love.'

'Not even one. I was just thinking that this was probably one of the best decisions I've ever made in my life.'

'I will spend every one of my days making you happy and you will never wish you had chosen differently.'

She wriggled around in his arms to face him. 'I can't imagine ever wishing I'd chosen differently. Thank you for being you.'

'And thank you for choosing me.'

He kissed her tenderly and she'd never felt safer and happier in her life.

'OK, lady. You have to be up bright and early to teach your first craft workshop tomorrow. How exciting. Come on, let's go to bed.'

'IS IT ON?' Debs tapped the screen. 'Bloody Portuguese WiFi!'

'Can you hear me?' Fiona fiddled with the volume controls on her iPad.

'Are we all here? Can you see me?' Samantha peered into the camera on her phone. A little furry face appeared behind her on the screen and they all laughed. 'I have someone to introduce to you later, ladies.'

Liv raised her G&T to the screen, where she could see all four of them on a joint call. 'I bloody love you girls. I'm proposing a toast to all of us. To the past and to the future. And to friendship! And I have decided that we should go on a cruise for our seventieth birthdays! *To us*.'

If you'd like to keep up to date with my latest releases, just sign up at the link below. We'll never share your email address and you can unsubscribe at any time.

Sign up here!

www.kimthebookworm.co.uk

Books by Kim Nash

Amazing Grace
Escape to Giddywell Grange

A letter from Kim

I do hope you enjoyed reading Sunshine and Second Chances. If you did enjoy it, and want to keep up to date with my latest releases, sign up at the following link. Your email address will never be shared and you can unsubscribe at any time.

Sign up here!
www.kimthebookworm.co.uk

I've really loved writing Sunshine and Second Chances and hope you have enjoyed a trip to Portugal with Liv, Debs, Samantha and Fiona. The Algarve, is one of my most favourite locations and we've enjoyed many holidays there and made lots of wonderful memories.

If you enjoyed Sunshine and Second Chances, I would be super grateful if you were able to write an Amazon review. I'd love to hear what you think, and it makes such a difference helping new readers to discover one of my books for the first time.

I also love hearing from my readers, so please do get in touch.

www.kimthebookworm.co.uk
www.facebook.com/KimtheBookworm
www.twitter.com/KimtheBookworm
www.instagram.com/kim_the_bookworm

Amazing Grace

Buy now!

She's taking her life back, one step at a time...

Grace thought she had it all. Living in the beautiful village of Little Ollington, along with head teacher husband **Mark** and gorgeous son, **Archie**, she devoted herself to being the perfect mum and the perfect wife, her little family giving her everything she ever wanted.

Until that fateful day when she walked in on Mark kissing his secretary – and her perfect life fell apart.

Now she's a single mum to Archie, trying to find her way in life and keep things together for his sake. Saturday nights consist of a Chinese takeaway eaten in front of the TV clad in greying pyjamas, and she can't remember the last time she had a kiss from anyone aside from her dog, **Becks**...

Grace's life needs a shake up – fast. So when gorgeous gardener **Vinnie** turns up on her doorstep, his twinkling eyes suggesting that he might be interested in more than just her conifers, she might just have found the answer to her prayers. But as Grace falls deeper for Vinnie, ten-year-old Archie fears that his mum finding love means she'll never reconcile with the dad he loves.

So when ex-husband Mark begs her for another chance, telling her he's changed from the man that broke her heart, Grace finds herself with an impossible dilemma. Should she take back Mark and reunite the family that Archie loves? Or risk it all for a new chance of happiness?

A funny, feel good romance about finding your own path and changing your life for the better – readers of Cathy Bramley, Jill Mansell and Josie Silver will love this uplifting read.

Escape to Giddywell Grange

Buy now!

After having her heart broken by boyfriend Jamie, successful businesswoman **Maddy Young** threw herself into her career, not realising how she was neglecting her friends and family. But when she's made redundant from the job she loved so much, Maddy takes her wounded pride back to her childhood home – the village of Giddywell.

With time on her hands being the only thing that Maddy does have, when best friend **Beth**, needs help with her doggy daycare business at Giddywell Grange, she's the obvious choice to help out.

Soon, Maddy is swapping designer handbags for doggy poo bags and Jimmy Choo heels for wellies… and when she meets furry friend Baxter the Cockerpoo, Maddy learns that love can come from unexpected places.

With Beth's brother – and Maddy's schoolgirl crush – **Alex**, back from the States, she soon realises he still makes her heart flip. But when Jamie crashes back into her world, with an offer which looks too good to refuse, will Maddy go back to her old life? Or will she discover that the key to her future lies in making other people happy?

An uplifting romantic comedy that will warm your heart – perfect for fans of Cathy Bramley, Milly Johnson and Lucy Dillon.

Acknowledgments

First, I'd like to say a huge thank you to Lauren for your wonderful editorial advice and encouragement and also to Jon for your fantastic final polish and input. Your hard work is very much appreciated.

To Hannah, for holding my hand through the final part.

To Lisa/Mary Jane for creating the most gorgeous cover and to Lydia for being my sounding board on the cover.

Thanks to Ollie for your love and support. Love you to the moon and back, my not so little man!

To Lisa, for being my biggest book cheerleader and for telling everyone she meets about her little sister's books (which is sometimes a little embarrassing!)

To Roni for letting me go over plot holes and timeline issues while out walking through the countryside and apologies to all the mountain bikers and dog walkers who think I'm a loon wandering around talking to myself.

To Nicola May, for being a fab holiday companion on our trip to Portugal. I will never eat vegan food again without thinking of you! You know why!

To the blogger and author community that I chat to on a daily basis. I cannot tell you how much you mean to me and have spurred me on to keep writing. Your kind and funny comments, tweets, posts are an absolute joy.

To everyone at Bookouture. You are the best bunch of people I could wish to work with. Your talent, enthusiasm, positivity and energy is incredible.

And finally I'd like to thank my friends. The people who inspire me on a daily basis. Those who inspired me to write this story about friendship. I am so very fortunate to have such amazing friendships in my life and am surrounded by the most brilliant, bright, brave, funny, kind, loving, thoughtful and wonderful people that make my world complete.

Printed in Great Britain
by Amazon

36367793R00189